DOCTOR OLAF VAN SCHULER'S BRAIN

DOCTOR
OLAF VAN SCHULER'S
BRAIN

—— *by* ——

Kirsten Menger-Anderson

ALGONQUIN BOOKS OF CHAPEL HILL

2008

Published by
ALGONQUIN BOOKS OF CHAPEL HILL
Post Office Box 2225
Chapel Hill, North Carolina 27515-2225

a division of
Workman Publishing
225 Varick Street
New York, New York 10014

Stories in this collection originally appeared, in slightly different form,
in the following publications: "Reading Grandpa's Head" in the *Maryland
Review;* "The Baquet" in the *Southwest Review;* "The Story of Her Breasts" in
Plaztik Press; "The Doctors" in *Post Road;* "Salk and Sabin" in *Ploughshares.*

Library of Congress Cataloging-in-Publication Data
Menger-Anderson, Kirsten.
   Doctor Olaf van Schuler's brain / by Kirsten
Menger-Anderson. — 1st ed.
       p. cm.
   ISBN: 13-978-1-56512-561-2
   1. Medical fiction.   2. New York (N.Y.) — Fiction.   I. Title.
   PS3613.E486D63 2008
   813'.6 — dc22   2008026850

10 9 8 7 6 5 4 3 2 1
First Edition

— For my parents —

CONTENTS

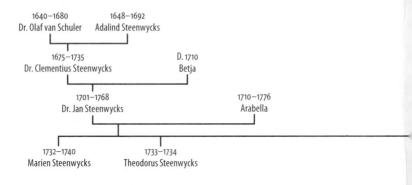

1640–1680
Dr. Olaf van Schuler

1648–1692
Adalind Steenwycks

1675–1735
Dr. Clementius Steenwycks

D. 1710
Betja

1701–1768
Dr. Jan Steenwycks

1710–1776
Arabella

1732–1740
Marien Steenwycks

1733–1734
Theodorus Steenwycks

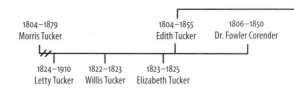

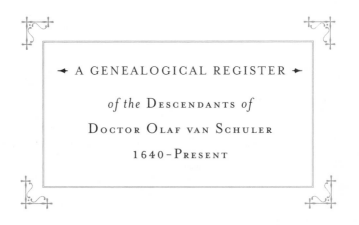

1804–1879
Morris Tucker

1804–1855
Edith Tucker

1806–1850
Dr. Fowler Corender

1824–1910
Letty Tucker

1822–1823
Willis Tucker

1823–1825
Elizabeth Tucker

❧ A GENEALOGICAL REGISTER ❧

of the DESCENDANTS *of*

DOCTOR OLAF VAN SCHULER

1640–PRESENT

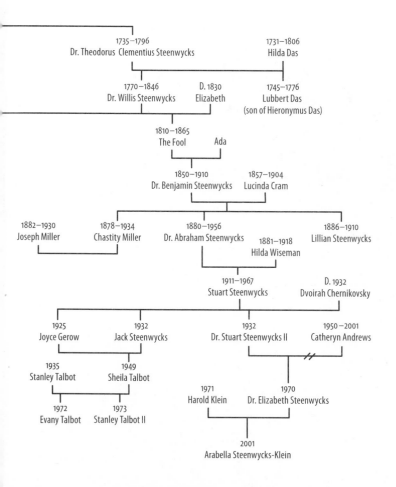

DOCTOR OLAF VAN SCHULER'S BRAIN

❧ Doctor Olaf van Schuler's Brain ❧

Doctor Olaf van Schuler, recently arrived in New Amsterdam with his lunatic mother, two bags of medical implements, and a carefully guarded book of his own medicines, moved into a one-room house near White Hall and soon found work at the hospital on Brugh Street. There, surrounded by misshapen bottles containing tinctures of saffron, wild strawberry, maple, and oil of amber, as well as more common tools of his trade — amputation saws, scalpels, sharpened needles, and long, painstakingly pounded probes — he indulged his peculiar perversion: slicing heads.

Mostly he studied the heads of pigs and cows, the latter of which had a brain that resembled the human one pictured in Dr. Galen's anatomy and was therefore of particular interest to the doctor. Late nights beneath the warm glow of the hospital's oil lamp, he unlocked his personal cabinet and marveled at the perfectly preserved, gray-pink tissue he'd sealed in glass jars of brine.

Had the Catholic Church not condemned his work, Olaf would have studied his brains during the day as well. But propriety compelled him to conceal his true passion and instead care for his mother, his patients, and his small bed of medicinal herbs. Mornings, when obligation did not busy him, he sat at Geert's Inn. Under the low wood ceiling, he pressed his forehead to his hands and thought about the brain and the human soul until his musings formed words, spoken words, like "animal spirits" and "the phlegm in man's head," which he repeated until the innkeeper said, "Beg your pardon?"

"The phlegm in man's head." Olaf blushed, his pale skin bursting with a pink that colored the dark circles beneath his eyes. His high forehead had led most of New Amsterdam to conclude that he had a large heart as well. And despite his odd outbursts and solitary conversations, his behavior confirmed this opinion. He was always willing to make late-night house calls and attend to the penniless when they complained of boils, headache, or gangrene. Unlike his predecessors — sullen young doctors who had crossed the Atlantic in search of a better life — Olaf even made an effort to treat the farm animals. "Forgive me," he said.

"It's that time," Geert chuckled. "Tonight's moon will be big as an udder. Best to stay in today. There's nothing but wickedness afoot this time of the month."

"I have work," Olaf said. "Two cases of fever and a child with a broken clavicle. And a call out to Bouwerie Lane to look at a cow."

Geert patted the doctor's shoulder. "Take good care."

"Don't touch me!" Olaf realized that he sounded like his mother; the strain of her care still lingered in his body.

"It's the moon. She gazes upon us, even now." Geert stepped away from the table, and Olaf, wondering if he should apologize again, gazed after him. Olaf had already felt the moon's effect. Just before sunrise, his mother, wielding a skillet, had broken through the wood wall at the back of their house. He'd been forced to bind her wrists with twine before locking her in the crate he'd built for her. He feared the strength of her madness would find expression in her hands and shoulders, allowing her to escape and run through the streets. Already the neighbors spoke in hushed tones when he passed by; he sensed that they suspected what he alone knew, that his mother was not merely feverish, as he'd claimed upon their arrival.

ON HIS WAY HOME from the inn, Olaf stopped at the bakery on Marktvelt to buy a loaf of white bread and two of the sweet currant rolls his mother liked. Rumor held that the shop's fresh-baked loaves fell short of the mandated two pounds, but the colored glass above the door, the smell of sugared raisins and ginger, and the baker girl's plump red lips always lured Olaf inside.

"We have fresh dark bread, still hot." Adalind Steenwycks smiled from behind the counter. Flour covered her neck and egg yolk stained her apron. She wore her hair in two thick braids.

"No," Olaf said, though he lingered by the counter staring helplessly. Even if she were not married, what would she want with him? A bachelor at twenty-four. A man who cut his own hair, as well as his mother's. A man who had learned to darn socks and make stew and pea soup. A man whose cares cut across his forehead in deep lines that pressed into a constant frown.

"How is your mother?"

"Well," Olaf lied.

"I thought I might call on her." She reached over the counter to hand Olaf the bread. "I don't mean to be forward."

"She prefers solitude."

"She has such a — such a goodness about her. Won't you bring her on Sunday?"

Olaf nodded, though he'd ceased going to church, not for want of faith — he prayed to the same God his neighbors did — but for the men who failed to have faith in him, men who watched a sick baby die and called it God's will, and who called the search for a cure devil's work. Even Olaf's only colleague, Dr. Johannes le Sueur, who owned not a single book and worked exclusively with urine to diagnose disease, knew nothing of Olaf's studies. Had he known of the brain experiments, he might have reported them to Petrus Stuyvesant of the Dutch West India Company, who certainly would have run Olaf out of town, as he'd done with the Quakers and had tried with the Jews. Olaf could say nothing — must say nothing.

"Send her my regards," Adalind said as Olaf turned homeward, carrying his warm packages as he might a sick child, gently, but far from his body.

OLAF ENTERED HIS HOUSE, hesitant to follow the narrow path that wound between the stacks of dishes, burlap sacks, cast off garments and precious belongings: a dried peony root, a small wooden box of ground pearls, his father's Bible, his mother's collection of carved wood saints. At home, Olaf lost his need for order, or the will to impose it. The disarray was foreign, yet comforting, a state that nearly convinced him that the place was not his, that he and Olaf were two different men, one destined for truth, the other only darkness.

"Adalind sends her regards," he said to his mother.

He tried to place a roll between his mother's tied hands, but it slipped from her fingers and fell. She had grown thinner as her illness became more pronounced. Her hair, once full and auburn, was now brittle and gray. A long red scratch, still moist with curative honey, ran down her left thigh.

When he was home, he sometimes released her so she could pace the thirty-foot length of their single-room dwelling, or kick the straw pallet he slept on. He let her shuck the corn that grew wild in the small lot behind their back door, and stir empty iron pots, which he set up on the dining table. She liked tangled yarn. He left bundles — in every color — on the floor amidst the clutter. He recited scriptures to her, knelt with her in prayer, and said nothing when she woke late at night to call upon God and plead for forgiveness.

"She's a whore," his mother muttered through the wooden bars of her cage. Today, he would not even untie her hands, though she looked up at him as a dying creature might, searching for meaning or relief. When he returned her stare, he comforted himself with his medical training: the watery, soulful appearance of her gaze was no more than the light on the clear, protective coating of the flesh of her eyes. She did not feel shame because she was mad. She did not feel trapped or sorrowful; she had lost the faculties of reason. She did not hate or love, and would not until he could cure her.

"That's unkind."

"Whore!"

"Come," Olaf said. "Come, let me see your nails."

His mother's hand shook as she placed it in his, and he knew that the pull of the moon had not yet left her. "We'll file these later," he said. "We'll take care of you later, once you've calmed down."

The soft, September sun cast a broken rectangle of light through the one transom window. Olaf again tried to hand his mother bread.

"I had breakfast at the inn," he said. "I've had my bread. It was a long night, and tonight will be also. But I'm getting closer. Very close to a cure, dear, dear Mother."

DOCTOR OLAF VAN SCHULER was born Olaf van Dijk in a small coastal town outside Amsterdam. His father died during childbirth — his heart failing as he sat powerless beside his wife who thrashed with the pain of her contractions. Olaf's Uncle Joris said the madness started that day, that his sister began to decline the moment her son was born. But he shared this thought only much later, after the madness was undeniable and nothing the minister did could dispel the demons from her soul.

A quiet, studious child, given to fits of anger, Olaf preferred the company of adults to children. He enjoyed the shipyards and spent hours watching arriving vessels. He claimed he would grow up to be a sailor, even practiced the seaman's swagger and, once, the seaman's foul mouth. He learned to tie knots — slipknots, square knots, figure eights. Clove hitch, bowline, sheet bend. He worked rope till it frayed and then wove it into the kind of bracelets he'd seen the sailors wear. Had fever not struck him the winter of 1651, he might well have followed through with his childhood plans. But during his convalescence he learned the pleasure of books, and he spoke so often to the doctors that he soon forgot the swarthy sailors and applied himself to medical science.

Filled with hope and the thrill of saving others as he himself had been, Olaf moved to Amsterdam, where he and his mother shared a two-room abode near the medical school. His mother's health continued to deteriorate, and he began to take over her work: preparing meals, tidying, hanging laundry. He had hoped her condition would improve — that the move to Amsterdam would relieve her deep melancholy, a malady that would pass as she grew familiar with her environs, or that with the help of God, she'd find strength to rid herself of the devil that sometimes raged inside her. As his studies enlightened him, he realized that matters were more complex.

Olaf began his study of the brain in 1662, two years before he was forced to leave Holland. He sliced open the heads of dogs, fish, lobsters, snakes, and chickens. He saw what other scientists had seen: that the brain was connected to the extremes of the body by a series of strings, and that the soul must rely on those strings to impart its will. The soul lived in the head, not in the heart, and bodily sickness could prevent its flow. Violence, anger, madness — all were symptoms of the soul's mortal conduit. All were conditions he could remedy, as soon as he learned how.

He tended to his mother dutifully, mixing tinctures of herbs and metals, which he spooned between her lips, sealing her mouth with one hand and stroking her throat with the other to make sure she swallowed. She seemed most lucid after a simple mix of wine and dry tobacco, a well-known curative that Olaf refined and recorded in his medicine book. He began to treat cases of fever and head-ache, for neighbors mostly, who knew of his art. News of his medicines spread, and he was gaining a reputation as a skilled alchemist when the incident changed everything.

The day had been unusually hot, though it began as most other days did, with Olaf rising to find his mother in tears.

"Henrick, Henrick," she repeated. The name not of her dead husband, but of a cow she'd grown fond of when she was a child.

"Good morning, Mother," Olaf said. He examined her skin and lips for any sign of rash or abrasion, sniffed the glass jar of urine she'd filled for him, poked the fleshy part of her arm to see how her body responded, searching, as always, for signs that his latest cure had improved her condition.

"I have two hands," she said. "Two hands."

"Indeed you do." He took his mother's trembling hands in his and pressed her fingers to warm them.

She surprised him with a bite on his shoulder.

"Come now, Mother dear," he said. She had not bitten or struck him in months, leaving him to believe that he had mastered the violent symptom of her madness with a mix of ground millipede and mercury. Now he was no longer sure.

He helped her dress and then tended to his own attire: the usual breeches, coat, and feathered hat. He prepared a breakfast of sliced bread with preserves, and explained to his mother that he had four appointments that morning. He did not mind that she looked past him to the bare wall of their home, or that she traced the deep lines she'd scratched into the wooden tabletop.

Looking back, he wondered if the heat was to blame, or the fact that he felt preoccupied by the dull pain where his mother's almond-colored teeth had nearly broken through skin. He wondered if the preserves had gone sour, or the bread, allowing a poison to find his blood. He had not been himself, could not even remember rightly.

He'd walked down Hoogh Street, his box of tinctures beneath one arm, his bleeding knives in a leather bag, which he swung absently as he turned right, then left, at last arriving at Jeremias Smits's home, where the bedridden Jeremias awaited. He'd sliced open the skin of the frail man's fingertips, a routine bleeding, and advised him to avoid organ meats and all things pulled from the ground. He then wiped the blood from his knife.

His previous visits had ended here, with a professional nod and a kindly word or two about the weather. Olaf must have remarked about the heat as he wrapped linen around the man's fingers to stop the blood. He must have noted how unseasonable it was, how the crops would surely be affected. Perhaps he even wiped the moisture from the old man's forehead. But he remembered only waking, hours later, as if from a stupor, the old man dead beside him, his bleeding unstopped. Fear commanded the doctor's hands. He rolled Jeremias's body in a long winter cloak. The corpse could not remain where the old man's daughter would find it when she next called. He panicked. How could he have failed at so simple a treatment? What had he done? What of his reputation? What of the body itself? He could not carry it through the street in broad daylight, though this is exactly what he did, cradling the wrapped corpse in his arms, his eyes wild with fright.

He might have escaped undiscovered had he not carried the corpse to his home, where he decided to slice open the skull. A human brain, a brain that had actually housed a soul, would further his studies. He would make up for the man's untimely death by naming his cure for Jeremias.

But then Olaf's mother was beside the corpse, screaming, and the neighbors came to check on her, and what they found so disturbed them that they ran from the front door screaming as well.

Olaf wiped the blood from his hands and face, gathered his tinctures and medical notes, along with a few of his mother's belongings and, leaving the half-opened skull on his bedroom floor, guided his mother to the docks, where he sternly bid her to remain until his return. Luck was on his side, as the *Broken Heart* was leaving for New Amsterdam that afternoon, and under the name Olaf van Schuler, the doctor booked two passages.

THE FULL MOON made Olaf nervous, for he, too, could feel the pull of the heavenly body. His senses heightened—he could smell the lichen that grew beneath his floorboards and the mold on the bread left out for the pigs in the street. He could hear the sigh of his bedclothes, the whisper of the words in his notebooks, the echo of clanging saucers and spoons he'd put away hours before. When he ran his fingers through his hair, he could almost feel his brain, as if the organ were raw and exposed. He touched his scalp, gently rubbed. Since arriving in the colony, he had experienced four stupors, all of which descended upon him at home. Only time stood between him and another public bout of illness, or worse, another incident.

"Mother," he said, but she was now sleeping, her head tucked close to her chest, her fingers splayed over bent knees. She was sitting, back pressed to the wall. Her shadow, hunched and dark, could belong to a demon, and on the full moon, Olaf thought it might.

"Mother," he said again. He wanted her to open her eyes and say that she would recover. He prayed — the words running fast through his head — that sense and sanity would return to carry away his troubles. But his mother only smiled, her lips an empty arc. "I must attend to my patients," he said, and if she heard, she did not respond.

HIS FEET HEAVY as he strolled along Smits Vly to visit Farmer Janssen's cow, Olaf worried that he had not taken enough rest before departing for his rounds. The dirt road was soft after the late-summer thundershowers. The air smelled of sheep dung and ripening apples. He paused to rifle through his medicine bag, pulling out a dented tin of tobacco. A teaspoon or two between his cheek and jaw would do the trick — raise his spirits, dispel his dread. Beside the road, a wolf, recently shot and left to decompose as a warning to his kin, caught his eye. If he succeeded in saving the cow, he could always take the wolf head back to the hospital for the evening's studies.

The cow, however, did not survive. She was dead upon his arrival.

"Nothing we can do for her now," Janssen said, accepting Olaf's sympathetic hand.

"She has some meat on her," Olaf noted and, proffering his usual excuse, that his mother made a fine stew from the brains of the cow, offered to buy the head. He could leave it on the street in front of his next patient's home — no one would steal it — and then take it to the hospital, where he could saw it apart.

"You shall have it," Janssen said, removing his ax from the stable wall.

OLAF AND THE COW head arrived at the hospital just before nine, when the inns and taverns closed their doors, and the denizens of New Amsterdam abandoned their empty glasses and cards and backgammon games to return home to bed or a nightcap of West Indian rum. Had he arrived at the iron-braced door any later, he would have had to wait for the streets to clear before he stepped into the hospital. But as long as he entered before the mandated closing time, he could confidently assume he'd passed unobserved.

Inside, he set the head on the plank floor and felt for

a candle and tinderbox. Even in the moonlight that crept through the shuttered hospital windows, Olaf could discern that Dr. Johannes le Sueur had left the space in disarray, abandoning pints of urine on the central table and leaving a broken glass and its pungent contents spilled on the floor. Why could his colleague not attend to his own debris? As he lit the candle and then the gas lamp and set to work with the broom, anger and dismay coursed through his muscles.

He had to rest for a moment, breathe deeply and exhale before he could take up his saw. He bit his tongue so pain would keep him focused. He should leave the work for tomorrow morning, early, when he felt rested; he should return home, to his mother, who must be hungry. But the thought of his mother, her hands still tied, her wide eyes gazing into his, forced his hand. She was failing.

Bone crumbled beneath his saw as the pale mass of the cow brain unfolded before him. Into the center he drove two probes. He knew the texture and composition and where to find the pineal gland. He'd mixed its tough meat with dozens of tinctures, observed the effect on color, size, and elasticity, and noted the mixtures that appeared promising. The answer was there in the body before him.

"Olaf! By God."

In the doorway stood Dr. Johannes le Sueur, dressed in his good jacket and crowned hat, just in from a stroll, it seemed. He was not a man to welcome spilled animal blood, particularly on the night of the full moon.

Turning from the gray-green gland squeezed between his probes, Olaf saw not a man but a monster, an apparition with cruel eyes and clawed hands that could steal what remained of the night.

"You must let me continue," he said.

"What devil's work is this?"

Johannes shut the door and stepped closer. In his hand he held a walking stick, slightly raised, Olaf thought. The metal orb at the top caught the gaslight.

"What we have is the soul," Olaf said. "The seat of man's soul."

"What you have is a cow skull. Cows have no soul."

"But here — here before you —"

Olaf wanted to tell him about Descartes, about the work that medical men were doing abroad. He wanted to show his piss-prophet colleague what the new science taught, and he wanted his colleague to turn around and go home, or rather, not to have arrived at all. But he could say none of it. He felt the heat in his cheeks, a twitch in the muscle of his shoulder. The gland fell from between his silver implements.

Johannes stepped forward, and again Olaf tried to form words. Johannes would tell Stuyvesant; Stuyvesant would ban Olaf from the colony, or worse, discover the past that had driven him to New Amsterdam's shores. Where would he go? How would he study?

"Away!" Olaf cried, though it was he, and not Johannes who was leaving. The two men passed each other, Johannes moving slowly, walking stick extended in self defense; Olaf armed only with an animal impulse, flight. He grasped the door frame for support. Moonlight spoiled the darkness, lightened it so he could not wear its disguise. Still, he turned and ran, deep into the night.

WHEN OLAF AWOKE, he was lying prone in front of the stone church near the waterfront. His shirt had torn and he'd lost both shoes and stockings. Rocks pressed the soft upper arch of his feet. The skin of his right arm was broken and bleeding in four lines of red fingernail scratches. His clothes smelled of the ocean, of drying sea bass and slippery brown bladder wrack. He clutched a handkerchief, Adalind's, the cloth filthy, but still perfumed with nutmeg and cinnamon. Around him fragments of cream-colored eggshell littered the ground. A line of ants disappeared beneath the one step leading to the church door. Night had passed leaving only the effects of forgotten moments. Why had he come here? Had he spoken to Adalind? What twisted path had led him to this spot?

"Have you come for food?" In the doorway stood the

schoolmaster who was conducting services while the minister returned to Holland to attend to his ailing father. A fringe of blond hair encircled his bald head like a halo that had slipped a few inches too far. "You needn't kneel," he continued. "Is it water you need?"

Olaf knew the schoolmaster from the few Sunday sermons he'd attended months earlier. The schoolmaster, despite his kind voice and smile, did not seem to recognize him.

"Come inside." The schoolmaster extended a hand. He stepped forward, past the eggshells and the handkerchief Olaf did not remember dropping.

"I am mad," Olaf said. He brushed the dirt from his palms. His time in New Amsterdam was done. Other men, great men, would carry on his studies. Not Johannes le Sueur, not this man of God, and not Olaf — certainly not Olaf. He might find refuge in another town, build a new practice, care for his mother for as long as he could. But he had no time to find the cure.

"Come inside," the schoolmaster said again. "Men can only do so much."

"We can heal the soul," Olaf answered. "We have the power."

Then he accepted the outstretched hand, because faith alone did not grant him the strength to rise.

❧ The Burning ❧

Richard Shaftsbury lit the fire and then a single candle. In the early days, the first days of his marriage, he and Gardenia burned dozens of candles before she returned to the kitchen and he set out lines of silver tankards. Tallow had flowed like ale, and the tavern had the warmth of expectations: they'd build a mahogany bar, stencil flowers above every door, serve chocolate, from London, which Gardenia had seen once. The King's Inn, they'd called it, raising the carved wood sign. Now, four years later, only the soft light of the evening's candle held promise.

The one early customer sat across from Richard, though Doctor Clementius Steenwycks never paid a cold shilling for his evening libations. People whispered that he was as odd as his father, who pickled animal heads and sliced them apart until he lost his reason entirely. He'd raped a woman — Clementius's mother — in the shadows of the docks where she awaited her young husband, a man who raised Clementius as a son, despite a shroud of rumors and ignominy. As a youth, Clementius found love only with the feebleminded daughter of a blind locksmith, and she bore him one son, Jan, now grown and gone, before she succumbed to fever.

"Raining again," Clementius said, silk robe parted over narrow chest, pipe filled with Indian tobacco. His eyes, a peculiar hazel that appeared to change hue as his gaze shifted — first to Richard, then to the kitchen, then to the smoke rising before him — had a self-satisfied glimmer, as if the doctor had peered into himself and found everything in perfect order. Though his shoulders hunched awkwardly, a symptom of long nights of study, he remained fit and well groomed. "Are you ready?"

Richard nodded. Rain kept all but the rowdiest drinkers away, and the night promised brawls. On rainy nights, he thanked the Lord for bringing Doctor Clementius Steenwycks to his inn, thanked the Lord that he had a medical man on hand, and one willing, on occasion, to snatch drunkards from their stools and thrust them into the darkened streets. Most evenings Richard bemoaned the fact that he'd let his two best rooms to Clementius for half their worth. He'd thought the doctor's practice would bring business. Never once did it occur to him that the practice would never be large, or that the few patients who arrived each day would feel too sick for lime punch and whiskey.

Clementius pushed his half-empty cup across the table. Tonight he would stitch broken lips and wrap bruised arms and bent fingers — tasks beneath a doctor with vast experience and interests, but which Richard respected far more than the strange remedies imported from London or the careful studies the medical man did on the hogs in the New York streets. Clementius had curious interests, but then, he was an unusual man.

"Perhaps Gardenia will prepare roast beef?" Clementius said, a demand more than a question. The doctor would eat and drink as he pleased tonight. The fact that Gardenia was indisposed and unable to cook did not matter. "And an apple crisp with cream."

Richard wiped the tabletop with the torn cuff of his shirt. What bothered him more than the menu, which would keep his lovely servant girl in the kitchen all evening, was the gnawing certainty that the doctor had requested the dishes for exactly this reason. Richard should never have confided in Clementius. But the two had spent so many evenings in the flickering light of the tavern that the innkeeper had at last broken down and admitted everything: his wife, Gardenia, was a drunk who belched unwomanly odors. She drank whiskey with breakfast and swallowed great gulps of rum for supper. The last time she'd tended to tallow, she'd left the task unfinished and the tavern dark for several nights. The time before, she'd made soap, the bars harsh and misshapen. After bathing with them, the lodgers broke out in rash, leaving the doctor to attend to the scabrous skin with mineral tonics. Her bread did not rise; her porridge never thickened; she left trousers and socks on the line long enough that the wind made them filthy. She failed to attend to her appearance or that of the tavern. Richard hired the servant girl because Gardenia wouldn't — couldn't — help. Wasn't there some justice in that? Some right of man to small pleasures?

The doctor, clean-shaven chin jutting out at an unappealing angle, had admitted the possibility, had noted that the servant girl was indeed comely, and had discussed the matter with the butcher, cordwainer, cooper, and a whole crew of mariners before Richard promised a reduced monthly rent in exchange for the doctor's discretion. Though Richard did not mind bedding the servant girl while Gardenia lay passed out on the kitchen floor, he shuddered to imagine his wife's reaction if she heard tell of it. All the traits that first drew him to her — her strength, her will, her violent temper — would become sharp, devouring teeth. He'd emerge bloodied and broken, if at all.

"Richard!" Gardenia's voice rose from the dirt-floored cellar, where earlier that day she'd fallen and decided to remain. She'd called for a blanket, which Richard provided, and then asked for a towel. How she ordered him about! When she had been well, managing her share of the inn's tasks, he hadn't minded. He'd loved her girth and the awkwardly curved seams in the dresses she sewed herself. He loved the dark, empty rectangle where she'd lost a tooth in a childhood fight. He loved, once loved, the woman whose thick layer of fat now protected her from the otherwise intolerable dampness of the cellar floor. "Bring some bread and molasses," she called.

Outside, thunder rumbled — soft, yet promising to near and rage. Richard sighed. The cellar was off the kitchen and down a half flight of wooden steps, far closer to the bread than where he now stood.

"The girl will fix dinner," he said to Clementius before turning to his wife's demands. "Whatever you please."

As EXPECTED, THE night brought nothing but ruffians — mariners mainly, in baggy tar-covered breeches and heavy wool coats — men accustomed to water and storms, who paid before drinking, for none would serve them otherwise. They sang loudly of ships that became women, of masts that tickled the sky, and of whores who waited on the lower decks promising honey and lime juice. Their ship had docked two days ago. Hard-earned shillings still clinked in their pockets.

Richard poured round after round of cider and punch. His head ached, and rum soaked his shirtsleeves. He was the ale master; his world was measured in pitchers and pints. And with the servant girl trapped in the kitchen over apple crisp and Gardenia asleep in the cellar and the demands for refills piling upon him in rapid succession, he discharged hard cider with a sloppiness that left the floor awash in alcohol and mud.

Clementius, who usually retired to his rooms after dinner, remained in the tavern, appearing almost saintly in his night robe. He'd moved near the fire and now bent over a pile of medical journals obtained at an exceedingly high cost from the Continent. He studied these often, sometimes sharing a highlight with Richard: an obscure case of frogs in a child's stomach, a grandmother who birthed a wild duck, a man who'd grown seven thumbs. "I've seen no such wondrous things in New York," he'd say mournfully. "Not a one."

A plate crashed against the floor. Richard turned from the bar, but not in time to tame the first of the evening's disruptions.

"A pound of yams? A pound of yams!" The screaming mariner had a scar that ran from jaw to ear and likely beyond, concealed by tufts of lousy brown hair. He rose from his stool, legs uncertain, arms braced to fight.

"Coward!" The opponent had been to the King's Inn before and had a limp to show for it. "Fool!"

"I'll eat no more yams!" The first punch fell like a dead branch from a tree, inevitable but without force.

"None of that." A third man rose, but Richard already stood between the fighters, his hand outstretched, palm raised.

"A shilling for the plate," he said.

The night was young and the mariners not too drunk to reason. Richard closed his fingers over the handful of coins. The mariners glared at him, their stubbled chins defiant. In the old days, the early days, Gardenia quelled the fights. None would strike a woman, and one of her icy blue stares would silence even the meanest rogue.

Over the filth and demon rum came the scent of baked apple. Richard turned to the kitchen, to the haven where he knew the servant girl stood. The mariners, the foulmouthed men, could wait.

"Two helpings," Clementius called after him. "Ask the girl to bring . . ."

"She'll not come out here!" Richard did not mean to raise his voice. He hadn't even realized how angry he was until that moment.

"Is this gratitude?" Clementius said. "I spend good money

for the latest research from France and Holland and Austria, to ensure your health. I sit here now, prepared — "

"Two helpings," Richard said. "With cream."

In the kitchen, he set his pitcher aside. Bowls of dried plums and West Indian molasses sat behind a plateful of softening butter and a halved loaf of bread. The servant girl picked baked sugar from the top of her apple crisp. Above her, the sheet of hand-blocked French wallpaper, which Gardenia had purchased at great expense from the booksellers, had blackened and begun to peel.

"Angel," Richard said. Behind him, the bar hummed softly, far away. "My little angel."

The servant girl turned, guilty smile radiant. "I didn't hear you, sir."

He stepped closer and cupped her chin in his palm.

She contemplated him, raised two sticky fingers to trace the lines of his face. "You look tired," she said.

He bent forward to kiss her, felt her thinness. He could lead a happy, balanced life with her by his side. He pulled her closer. His hand found her neckline, the soft, warm skin of her breast.

"The apple bake," she said.

"It will wait." Now that passion had woken, he could not bear to return to the tavern. He lifted the girl easily, pressed her back to the wall. "Angel," he said, trousers dropping round his feet before he reached forward to push up her skirts. He felt her thighs tense as she stretched her legs. He thought he heard her giggle. A skillet slipped to the floor. Hanging bunches of lavender and horehound struck the wall with the lovers' rhythm. "Angel!" he cried.

Hardly a minute had passed. A giddy minute. A wonderful minute. A minute in which Richard felt more pleasure than he had in months. He would come to the kitchen again, he decided. He would take refuge in the servant girl. He would hold her, stroke her, kiss her. His cheeks flushed, his breath came hot and quick. He listened to the screaming for a full breath before he realized that the voice belonged to Gardenia.

"Fiend!" she screeched. "Monster!"

Richard turned; the servant girl slid to the floor. Gardenia, red hair colored with vomit, glared at them. Her skin had hardened into numerous deep wrinkles, her lips hung slightly apart. She'd come for the baked apple, Richard realized. The smell had drawn her, a dumb beast to a heavenly trough. He hated her. Hated the hands worn raw from years of dishes, and the burns on her arms from the stove. He hated that she failed to sew and cook and clean. He hated her thickness, her rum-sweat odor.

"Adulterer!" she yelled. Unsteadily, she turned toward the tavern. The servant girl shrieked, her almond curls freed from the cap that had fallen to the floor only moments before.

"Gardenia." Richard realized his wife would cause an uproar, provoking the men in the other room. But Gardenia had already pushed open the door.

"You will suffer for this!" she screamed over a chorus of derisive cries and catcalls. "Suffer till the end of your days."

Richard raced to her side and placed a restraining hand on her shoulder "Come here," he said. "Come down to the cellar."

THE SERVANT GIRL discovered the body. She'd gone down to the cellar for a pint of cream, she said later, though Richard suspected that she'd thought to beg Gardenia's forgiveness. Her scream, a mix of rending fear and surprise, brought him to the cellar with Doctor Clementius Steenwycks at his heels along with a stumbling group of drunken mariners.

"What is it?" Richard said, before his eyes adjusted to the dimness. Above his casks of pear and juniper wine hung thick clouds of smoke. The floor was covered with soot, so slippery that he nearly lost his balance — nearly tumbled into the fatty remains of his wife: a leg, stocking intact; a thumb; two fingers, one with a wedding band; and a few strands of hair.

"By God," Richard said. The darkness did not conceal

his disgust. He raised a trembling hand to his shoulder, pressed it over his heart. "Gardenia!"

"I've only read of such things," Clementius said. He breathed deeply, despite the foul stench, and turned to push the nearest mariner aside. "Away with you! All of you!"

The men might have persisted, might have forced their way into the room, had not their leader, a weathered sailor with a gut that had braved the fiercest storms, vomited. Those behind him retreated, a rush of uncertain feet and laughter from the men too far back to have seen the remains.

"Don't touch a thing!" Clementius commanded. He stepped into the room. "Bring a lantern!" he cried to the servant girl, who still crouched by the door, tears blinding her to the sight, perhaps even the stench of the room.

"Fetch it now!" Clementius said. The girl looked at Richard, who stared vacantly at his wife's one intact shoe. The flesh of Gardenia's foot still gave form to the cloth and the bronze buckle remained tightly fastened.

"She was drinking when I left her. She had a flask in one hand and a tankard of ale in the other. She was alive." Hands clasped, Richard might have fallen to his knees, save for the slime that covered the floor and reminded him of his dignity.

"A fiery death!" the doctor said. The tail of his night

robe swung as he shifted his weight, surveying the dim room. "And yet — the wooden barrels are intact. And the blanket." He ran a finger over the wall behind him where a mucuslike substance had begun to congeal.

"'Tis the curse of her family," Richard said, both hands now covering his tearstained cheeks. "Her father died in flames, and his father before him. The bedchamber caught fire. A curse. We are cursed!"

The doctor sniffed his fingers and held them aloft so that the dim light from the kitchen fire could illuminate them. "It's as I've read," he said. "Exactly as I've read."

"I loved her," Richard added. "Loved her with all my heart."

The bright light of a lamp, held aloft from somewhere in the kitchen and approaching rapidly, filled the room and confirmed that the slimy matter coating the floor and stone walls had a dull yellow cast.

Richard jumped back, nearly colliding with the doctor, who had turned to order the servant girl forward.

But the approaching figure was not the servant girl. Leading a half-dozen sailors, the constable stood twice as wide as the expected party, his shirt and slacks stuck fast to his skin, drenched by the night's driving rain.

"Richard Shaftsbury?" The constable's eyes found the innkeeper and never once turned to Gardenia's sole remaining leg, a fact that suggested that the lawman had been apprised of the situation and knew better than to stare directly at the dead woman. Behind the constable, the sailors leaned forward to watch the arrest. "You can come with me peacefully, or I shall be obliged to use force."

Lamplight drew his face in shadowed lines, and Richard, eyes locked with the constable's, believed he saw the outline of iron bars.

"I've done nothing," he said. But he did not resist when the constable took his shoulder and led him to the stairway.

Upstairs in the kitchen, the servant girl — perhaps hoping for an explanation, perhaps the answer to an unasked question — watched Richard as the constable charged an unthinkable crime: murder. Even the sailors remained silent.

"I must have the corpse," the doctor whispered before the constable yanked Richard away. "Promise me the corpse."

"What little remains," Richard said over his shoulder. "If it is mine to give."

"Your innocence is assured," the doctor said firmly. "Only science can explain the night's happening."

THE WEEKLY GAZETTE reported Gardenia Shaftsbury's grotesque death on the front page beneath the headline "His Bowells shall be Removed and Burnt," a punishment which the writer decided fitting for the crime. Not every one agreed, though most all of New York had an opinion. Some felt that Richard should be drawn and quartered; others felt he should hang. Very few knew about Doctor Clementius Steenwyck's investigation, or that the doctor adamantly maintained that Richard was not guilty.

The day of the trial dawned clouded and cold. Hoarfrost covered the cobblestones and icicles hung like blades from the boughs of the trees along Broadway. Only a small crowd amassed before the courthouse. Trials held less interest than executions, and that morning the weather encouraged many to remain beside fires. Most came merely to socialize and would disperse long before the proceedings finished.

Inside the Supreme Court of Judicature, the jury had assembled — men with grim faces and questioning eyes. The eldest, a white-haired man in a knee-length jacket, chewed a slab of smoked beef, which perfumed the room with hickory. The youngest, still red from a rigorous scrubbing, looked to be no more than eighteen. The magistrate had not yet entered, but the witnesses sat ready: the servant girl, four mariners, the constable, and Doctor Clementius Steenwycks.

Richard waited, as all accused men before him, across from the magistrate's bench. Long nights in prison had worn on the innkeeper, his clothing dusty and torn, his face gaunt, his eyes wild beneath unruly brows. He clasped his hands across his lap and looked neither to the left, where a guard ensured he would not escape, nor the right, where the doctor sat, as he'd promised, with a leather case thick with files.

When the magistrate entered, Richard stood. The clerk read the charge.

"The prisoner has submitted a written defense?" the magistrate asked, though he held the answer to this question, a single sheet of paper, between the fingers of his left hand.

Richard nodded, and the judge turned to examine the paper. One of the jurors nervously tapped the wooden bench, but otherwise the room remained silent.

"The hand is illegible," the magistrate declared at last, his eyebrows meeting to form a single dark line that crossed his pale forehead.

Richard examined the floor, which had discolored where the rains leaked through the ceiling. The court was not sealed. At any moment justice might escape, pounding through the alleys, the taverns, the inns, just as his illiterate heart now pounded, the beats so loud he could hear them echo. "I — " he began.

"Silence!" The magistrate lifted his palm. "We will hear from the first witness."

The constable stood, borrowed jacket pulling tight over his shoulders. He related the crime as it had been told him: Richard and Gardenia had fought. She'd run screaming through the tavern before her husband captured her and threw her into the cellar with force enough that the men in the tavern could hear the bones crack. The smell of burned flesh brought the men to the crime scene, where they beheld Richard bent over his wife's scant remains, an evil grin commanding his lips.

"And you witnessed these events?" the magistrate said.

"No, sir. But I have examined the —"

"Very good," the magistrate said. "You may sit down." He called each of the four sailors in turn, their testimony touching upon the number of drinks consumed that evening as well as the moment they'd first heard screams — two declaring that the sound had come early in the evening, and one admitting that he'd heard no screams. The fourth said the screams came after the remains had been discovered and that the wronged wife haunted the tavern.

Richard rested his face between uncertain hands. His knees, pressed together and exposed to the jury and judge, had locked.

The servant girl stood. She wore a dark gray gown, much finer than any she'd worn to the tavern. Her cheeks retained their crime-night pallor, but her lips shown red and plump. Kissable. Richard might have forgotten that he sat accused of murder had not distress commanded his thoughts. She spoke one-word answers to the magistrate's questions: Were you working the night of the crime? Yes.

Did you witness the murder? No. Do you believe Richard Shaftsbury innocent? Silence, then, "No, sir. I shan't return to the King's Inn, ever."

Richard raised a shaking hand to his heart, and the magistrate dismissed the girl with a wave.

Doctor Clementius Steenwycks now stood. He'd donned a smart frock coat for the occasion, and even the magistrate looked shoddy by comparison. The doctor's angular chin, which most people had dismissed as odd or severe, now looked authoritative, undeniable, strong. The doctor waved a finely trained hand, and his words filled the courtroom with confident calm. He spoke eloquent words, long words: alcohol saturation makes one flammable . . . fat causes the body to burn . . . intemperance . . . evidence from scientific journals . . . a case in the south of France.

"She has most certainly combusted spontaneously," he said, the passion of his testimony calling sweat to his brow. He took a medical journal from his bag, and the jurors watched him, jaws slack with amazement, as he began to translate an excerpt from a recent Dutch study. The reported victim had consumed four pints of sherry, he read, and soon thereafter combusted, leaving only a fatty, yellow-gold substance on the walls and floor.

The sailors nodded, their recollections of the cellar confirming the article's descriptions.

"This man must not hang for a crime that is no crime at all," the doctor concluded, and the magistrate accepted the doctor's statement with a thoughtful nod.

Richard turned to Clementius, years of small resentments — lost revenue and loosely shared secrets — torn from the dark cove where he'd harbored them. For a moment he felt even love for the doctor.

RICHARD RETURNED TO the King's Inn the next morning, a free man, though the brief time in prison had lent his features new angles, and he seemed older by some years. He poured two cups of cider and slid one across the table to Clementius.

"To justice," Clementius said. "And soon, very soon, I shall publish my findings."

Richard nodded, tossed his drink back and poured a second. Empty of customers, the tavern felt as if it hadn't been occupied for years. Daylight lit the room, illuminating only the unclean tables and the tracked mud covering the floors.

The servant girl would not return to the inn, and Richard surveyed the room with hours in mind: four to scrape and mop the floor, two to clean the dishes, three to prepare an evening meal. The tasks piled, too many for his weary hands.

"Aye," he said, deciding that one more drink might help.

By evening, he'd done no more than light a fire and wipe the rim of his own cup. He leaned against his wooden bar, resting a throbbing forehead in the palm of his left hand. The night sky stretched clear and cold, whiskey weather, and on past nights, the inn would have burst with customers. That night only Clementius arrived, forced to dine upon the crusty remains of a loaf of bread, which he found in the kitchen and sliced himself.

"Too much ale tonight?" he asked, and Richard glared at him. "Round town they're saying this place has a ghost." Clementius laughed, about to comment upon the ignorance of his fellow man, when Richard turned and unsteadily made his way to the kitchen.

"A ghost!" Clementius called after him. "Imagine!"

But Richard did not need to imagine. He clearly heard Gardenia's shrill cry, and when he closed his eyes, he saw her: coarse hair tangled, skin rough with unwashed dirt, eyes moist with an uncomprehending fear. He knew she lay in the cellar. She'd fallen again. She wanted ale, bread, and molasses.

"Yes, darling," he whispered. And he knew, for the first time since the burning, that he had not killed — could never have killed — Gardenia.

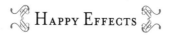 HAPPY EFFECTS

Constable Morris, already burdened with New York's most conspicuous gut, carried Nicolas into the Heathcote home on Bridge Street. Pale and limp, the cradled youth looked more like an unwashed linen than an eighteen-year-old merchant, though the boy did oversee the family business, counting wooden crates of sugar — white gold — as if they were already hard pocket currency. He'd left for the docks at sunrise, as his father once did, with a smile and a promise to return before sundown.

The clock struck one, the fine mahogany case vibrating slightly, and the boy's mother lay in bed dreaming of fur and brocade silk as she did most afternoons. She'd spent the morning bent over a metal tub pouring cups of strong tea and lemon water through her hair, a process that made her dizzy, but which the ladies assured would straighten the tight curls that had troubled her since childhood.

"Sarah Heathcote!" The Constable's voice roared through the parlor, reaching Sarah with an unwelcome harshness. Where was the servant girl? Why was the Constable, whose rasping breath was so well known throughout the South Ward that she recognized it from her bedchamber, standing in her front parlor?

She rose hastily, fastening her dress without her usual hooped petticoat and, pausing only to powder her face and apply a drop of rose oil, which she was certain made her seem youthful once more, stepped out to receive the Constable.

"My dear Mr. Morris," she began, but at the sight of her son draped limply in the large man's arms, she silenced.

The Constable brushed past her, laying the boy on the settee reserved for company.

"Nicolas!" She realized her voice had risen — she may have shrieked — her curls as unruly as the servant girl's. "Nicolas!" she called again, but the boy did not respond.

She took her son's hand between her palms. He had no visible injury, a few patches of black soot on his sleeve, nothing the servant girl couldn't brush away. And where was that girl? Why wasn't she here to bring water? That was all the boy needed. A glass of water.

"Nan!" Sarah cried. "Nan!"

Young Nan, hair fastened back in a tight white kerchief, dark skin covered in dust, emerged from the back of the house. Her cheeks were heavy, despite her lithe form, and she moved with the slow step of a much older woman. "I's sweeping the cobweb —" she began, but she stopped when she saw Nicolas stretched out on the settee.

"I'm very sorry." The Constable placed a hand on Sarah's shoulder. "I'm very sorry. He died in the fires."

"Mister Nicolas!" Tears streaked Nan's face, and she threw herself on the floor beside the body. "He pass, he pass!"

"Fetch some water," Sarah said, turning her head slightly, as if to brace herself against the girl's outpouring of sorrow. "We don't *know* he's dead. Not yet."

Nan, still sobbing despite Sarah's assurance, rose and raced from the room.

"They set fire to the stables," the Constable explained. "For days, the city has battled the blazes — one at the governor's house, another at the chapel, another at the Warren home, another at the docks. Only arson can account for them. And only one thing can account for the arson: the slaves are rising."

"To think," Sarah agreed. Her thoughts on the matter — that the Negroes had entirely too much freedom already and that the slave market on Wall Street, where all sorts of dark-skinned men entered New York, was too close to her home for comfort — required no further expression to be understood. She wrapped a sallow arm around her son's chest. His head, balanced unsteadily on the edge of the settee, rolled sideways, turning his gray-blue gaze toward the Constable. She remembered when the boy, a pale, perfect child, climbed the lip of the well and tumbled down — not into the well, which was covered of course, but onto the hard cobblestone. She'd run to him then, just as now. And he'd lain just as deathly, even more so, as the impact had drawn blood from his nose. But he had risen.

"Call the doctor!" Sarah cried.

The Constable, who must have realized that he was far more able to call upon a medical man than the tearful Nan, who'd returned with a brimming pitcher of water, stepped forward.

"Nicolas moved," Sarah explained. Nan, setting the pitcher on the side table and raising one sleeved arm to her nose, nodded her support. The Constable should know better than to make claims about life and its end. His job was to prevent death, not diagnose it. Medical matters were better left to medical men, and Sarah Heathcote knew exactly whom she needed. Not just any medical man would do.

"Fetch Doctor Steenwycks," she said firmly.

DOCTOR STEENWYCKS RUSHED through the front door of the Heathcote house, his rough-weave, floor-length cape and round brimmed hat, oddities that made the ladies titter, alive with the speed of his gait. Tall and gaunt, he could easily have lit the chandelier without resorting so much as to tiptoes, despite the fact that his shoulders stooped and his arms hung forward like some exotic monkey's. His narrow, pointed chin was reminiscent of his father's — a little-known medical man who lived and died above a ramshackle tavern.

"Jan Steenwycks," he said by way of introduction, nodding first to Sarah, then to Nan, who stood behind her mistress like a bashful child.

The doctor and Sarah had never met, though Sarah knew him from her Thursday night suppers. Since opening his practice two years earlier, and despite his dress and manners, he'd won the respect of the finest society. At dinner parties, he was known for his gracious toasts and long diatribes regarding the foolishness of his father's medicine. Witchery nonsense, he called it, not empirical science, and even old men whose only experience of doctors and medicine was the cures discovered in worn copies of *The Poor Planter's Physician* nodded. Doctor Steenwycks knew best. Only he could determine if a man were truly dead. Just last month the good doctor had pulled a drowned girl from the East River and brought her back to life with an air technique, the details of which the ladies were uncertain, though that did not stop them from vividly imagining the event. These days, no gentleman or lady was buried without a visit from Doctor Steenwycks, who was doing so well for himself that he'd purchased a large plot of land near Ranelagh Gardens and constructed a two-story home with a triangular pediment for his wife and young children.

The doctor dropped his walking stick, mahogany with mother-of-pearl insets, and bent low over Sarah's shoulder to examine the patient. "How long has he been so?" he asked.

Sarah, who had not moved from her son's side, stretched to read the grandfather clock that stood like a watchful soldier beside the sideboard containing her good china. "Three hours," she said, though it seemed only minutes ago that the Constable had set forth to fetch the doctor. Nan, who stood beside Sarah, addressed the doctor directly.

"You help Missus Heathcote now. It ain't right this."

She must have known it wasn't proper to address a white doctor — Nan knew her place — but the words fell from her lips with such tender conviction that even Sarah was touched.

"I should have been summoned at once." Doctor Steenwycks glanced about the parlor as if searching for a forgotten instrument. Satisfied, evidently, that he could discover nothing more from the room, he rested a thin, veined hand on Sarah's shoulder and not gently pushed her aside. With exacting precision, he placed an ear to Nicolas's chest and probed the boy's neck with the fingers of his left hand. "There is an absence of arterial pulsations," he declared without turning to address Sarah.

"He will recover then?" she ventured.

"Only if he is alive."

"Yes, yes. He was caught in the fires. But he has no markings — no burns. It was the Negroes who did it."

The doctor, who employed neither slave nor indentured servant and was rumored to frequent the taverns of ill repute on the outskirts of town where the black men congregated in blatant disrespect of the law, said nothing. For a moment Sarah feared she may have offended him, displeasing him enough that he would fail to treat Nicolas to the full extent of his wondrous abilities. Folding her hands in her lap and noticing the soot that had stained first her fingers and now her dress, she considered apologizing. Not a forthright apology, but a retraction, an acknowledgment that he might feel differently, though, really, how could people so black on the outside be anything other than black within?

"Have you a mirror?" the doctor said. Nan answered, her eyes on the floor. If Sarah's words troubled her, she showed no sign of it, except perhaps that she'd pulled deeper into her thoughts. "Yes, sir. I'll fetch it."

When she returned with Sarah's mirror, the doctor had already tried and abandoned his tins of smelling salts and sneezing powder and was busily engaged in inserting plugs of wool into Nicolas's nostrils. With a smile and a thank you that made Nan blush, Doctor Steenwycks took the hand-mirror and placed it before the boy's mouth. He appeared to examine himself for some minutes — Sarah expected that he'd pause to comb back his hair — but he set the mirror aside with a thoughtful frown.

"No sign of respiration," he said.

"Surely there is more you can do?" Sarah asked, recollecting the whispered remarks about the doctor's great powers. These few simple tests — hardly filling a quarter hour — could not be the substance of rumor.

"There are other techniques," the doctor said, "which may impart happy effects. I need vinegar, garlic, horseradish. Mortar and pestle. Have you onions?"

No sooner had Nan returned from the pantry, than the Constable appeared at the door.

"Mrs. Heathcote," he said, jacket nearly bursting over his heaving torso. Between two missing buttons, a swatch of tea-colored cloth poked out.

"Constable Morris." Sarah rose and stepped forward. The large man's presence comforted her, reminding her, even in these horrible times, that the world had order, enforceable laws, right and wrong.

"We've captured him!" the Constable managed between labored breaths. "The Negro arsonist."

Sarah smiled at the Constable, who appeared almost handsome as he spoke this good news. Behind her, Doctor Steenwycks removed Nicolas's shoes and poked the boy's feet with a long, sharp needle.

"Van Cortlandt's man." The Constable shook his head. "He will certainly hang. And if I may, I would myself escort you to the gallows."

Sarah had attended several public hangings, but never one to which she had so close a connection. Until that afternoon, crime had been only a topic she discussed with the ladies: the fact that Van Tilburgh slipped a strand of pearls from his host's dressing table, for instance, or that the Warrens had been burgled as they sat down to afternoon tea. She'd been a child the last time the slaves had risen, a mere child advised to avoid all black men and Catholics. And here she was, just turned forty, with a crime she could forever discuss with the ladies. A crime that she would laugh about as soon as Doctor Steenwycks revived Nicolas.

Doctor Steenwycks turned from his patient. "Bed linens," he said. "Several."

Nan ran off to the back closet where the good linens were stored. The Constable hovered in the doorway, his loss for words duly noted by Sarah who realized that the man might have intentions.

"We'll watch him hang. Isn't that right, Nicolas?" Sarah

said, turning to her son who now gazed at the ceiling with his lips stretched obscenely over cloves of garlic.

With a slight bow, the Constable excused himself, his retreating footsteps reminding Sarah of happier days. Days when her husband and Nicolas arrived home for the dinner the colored girl prepared. Days when the streets were safe from fires. Days when death belonged to other people, some of whom had most certainly been buried alive. If only she'd known the good doctor when her husband passed!

DOCTOR STEENWYCKS LEFT Nicolas swathed in bedsheets from head to toe. "There have been cases," he said beneath Sarah's demanding eye, "documented cases of the dead reviving." And yes, to be absolutely certain, one should wait for at least forty-eight hours before pronouncing the matter decided. And yes, he always recommended that his patients do just that. But for her own good, to protect her gentle nature, she must not lift the cloth. Not until he could reexamine the patient, which he did two days later, pronouncing the boy dead based on the appearance of livid spots. But Sarah would have nothing of it. No. No, in fact she had realized with increasing certainty as she sat on the chair she'd pulled to her son's unmoving side and Nan hovered behind her shoulder offering endless stories to "cheer the Missus," that her boy would not revive until his killer had been brought to justice. Or rather, she told herself in order to remain clearheaded, she could not with confidence confirm that her son had died until the murderous black man had been hanged — an event rapidly approaching and so anxiously awaited by the good denizens of New York that it had been moved from the courthouse to the Common to accommodate the expected crowd. "Wrap him again," she'd demanded, and the lean doctor had complied, admitting that a few more days would confirm, beyond all doubt, what he already suspected.

For those three days, Sarah sat by her son. Nan fixed tea and biscuits, fetched blankets, and carried the scented oils from the bedroom to the parlor, where Sarah applied them to her wrists and neck. She did not venture out even for her Thursday night dinner, and her absence alarmed the ladies, who called on her en masse the following day. But that afternoon, the Constable would be calling for her, and Sarah was concerned with her preparations and did not answer the door.

The execution drew Sarah from Nicolas's settee for the first time since the boy's return, and she considered her options carefully: pearls or silver? German serge or China taffety? All of New York would be watching her as she stood with her handkerchief unfurled and her hair piled in an exquisite tower by the Constable's ample side at the front of the wooden platform, now a full seven feet higher to provide a better view of this execution. She laced her girdle as tightly as her age-swollen fingers could manage, selected her broadest hooped petticoat, which she hoped would draw her waist narrow by comparison, and brushed her cheeks with a thick layer of powder that lessened but did not conceal her unladylike ruddiness.

"Nicolas," she said. He was her son, her fine, growing son who would one day marry a Van Cortlandt or a Beekman or some other society family. "Nicolas. Nicolas. Nicolas." She wanted to pull back the linen cloth, to hold his face between her hands. She wanted to explain to him that his assassin would soon be hanged and that he could rise safely and return to the warehouse, where things must certainly be in disarray. She leaned low over the prostrate form, her fingers hovering and ready to unfold the tightly wrapped cloth. Behind her, her husband's portrait regarded the scene with the green-blue the artist had chosen for his eyes. His skin had a gray cast, where the smoke from the unswept fireplace had discolored the paint, ash gray over Mediterranean olive. "Nicolas," Sarah said again. Nicolas would not recover until after the hanging. Pulling the sheet back now would be premature; pulling the sheet back now might ruin everything.

"Mrs. Heathcote." The Constable stood at the door,

which he'd taken the liberty of opening. "I — " He stopped as he took in the widow bent like a bird of prey over her son. Daylight made the room appear dark. Had Sarah not worn a heavy coat of perfumes, she too might have noticed the rancid odor that struck the Constable so hard he nearly stumbled. "Good heavens!" he cried. "Mrs. Heathcote."

"Why Constable Morris." Sarah straightened, clasping her hands behind her back. "How good of you to come."

Drawing a last breath of crisp afternoon air, the Constable stepped into the parlor. "The murderer will pay dearly for this. My poor, dear, S — " Though he began to speak her first name, he must have realized that such intimacy was inappropriate, for the word remained unsaid. "Shall we go, then?"

"Nan!" Sarah called.

The girl, who'd been sitting in the corner of the room, jumped, nearly toppling the bowl of peas she'd been shelling.

"Yes ma'am." Though she'd waited attentively on her mistress, Nan no longer shared Sarah's optimism. Her eyes were red with the tears Sarah would not allow herself, and she preferred to sit as far from Nicolas as the room allowed.

"I need you to sit with my son," Sarah said. "You're to offer him water if he wakes and to listen closely for any, for any . . . he's sure to be weak."

Nan nodded, though her lips pressed tight against horror. Sarah had not seen such fear in the servant girl's face since the day the child arrived with one change of clothes and the promise that she could card and spin. "Yes ma'am," she said.

Outside on the cobblestone pavement, the Van Cortlandt carriage — the finest in town, with its metal trim and high polish — stood loosely tethered. Though Sarah had condemned the carriage, as the other ladies had, for its high speeds and thoughtless presence on the city's narrow streets, she was more than happy to step, with the Constable's assistance, into the back and luxuriate on the soft pillows.

"How thoughtful," she said, "How very thoughtful."

"The Van Cortlandts insisted," the Constable said. "When they heard about your Nicolas."

Despite the cushioned seats, the ride to the Common upset Sarah's stomach, and the Constable had to demand that the carriage stop. Three times the carriage halted, and three times Sarah alighted with a kerchief to her face to cover the smile the gawking passersby brought to her lips. Everyone would soon know that Sarah Heathcote had ridden the Van Cortlandt carriage. The finest society would watch as she arrived at the hanging, delayed for her, with a nod and an offhanded comment about the violent rocking of the vehicle.

The Constable offered his thick, sweaty palm as a comfort, and Sarah took it as she listened to his stories of the new fires that raged near the docks. "The black plague," he said, "has descended upon us."

"I don't understand," Sarah said. "I just don't understand."

The carriage stopped, and she heard the expectant crowd, hitherto concealed by the crack of horse hooves and the clap of wheels on cobblestone and the warm immensity of the Constable. Hundreds had gathered across the green lawn of the Common that abutted Collect Pond. The black men were buried there — a fact not lost to the assembled masses, who whispered that the hanged man would be laid into the very ground he swung above.

The tavern keepers had shut their establishments and now stood among the most refined gentlemen in embroidered coats and silk stockings. Children ran between the vast skirts of their gossiping mothers. The tanners and blacksmiths, even the staff of McCully's Dry Goods Store, which had shut its doors and offered a holiday in honor of the occasion, stood out on the lawn vying for better views. Beside them, the British crew of the *Happy Tidings*, which had berthed that morning, leaving the sea-weary sailors scant hours to swallow a few pints of ale before following the barmaids to the Common, hollered and sang and spread rumors that the man who was about to hang had in fact been a dreaded pirate.

Into the crowd, head high, arm entwined in the

Constable's, swept Sarah Heathcote. She felt the eyes on her, heard her name in the surrounding murmur of voices — *the widow Heathcote . . . the Negroes have murdered her only son . . . how well she carries herself . . . such strength of character . . .* She turned neither right nor left as the Constable cleared a path for her, and she strode with dignified gait to the front of the crowd. Here she waited with the Constable, despite her expectations, for a full half hour before five stout wardens carried the prisoner, hands tied with a thick length of rope, onto the platform. The prisoner kicked and bit, his lips wide with curses, his eyes wild with fear and spite. And to think he'd once been with the Van Cortlandts!

"Oh, Sarah, he is the worst sort."

Sarah turned to find the ladies, rumpled from their fight to the front of the crowd. Faith and Margaret and Elizabeth and Mary, all wearing subdued grays and blacks.

"Well, you do look becoming," Faith said, though her tone made the compliment snide as she examined Sarah's finest green dress and pearls.

"Green suits her," the Constable noted.

Margaret took Sarah's hands between her own and squeezed, "We are so sorry to hear about Nicolas. Such a dear, sweet boy."

The wardens succeeded in righting the prisoner, who stood, with one warden at his legs to weigh them down and two more bracing his neck and back, directly beneath the crosspiece that spanned the lofting posts. The black man gazed forward, seemingly blind to the assembled audience and indifferent to the insults thrown from all sides.

"Nicolas," Sarah said. The heat of the crowd confused her. "Nicolas is home."

"We've taken a collection for his headstone," Margaret said.

"Oh, dear, no." Sarah felt suddenly panicked. "Nicolas isn't dead. Doctor Steenwycks —"

The wardens had the rope around the black man's neck. From where she stood, Sarah could have seen the veins that stood thick as string beans along either side of his throat. But she didn't turn to look. How could she watch the execution while Nicolas was rising? How could she have left her dear boy at home alone?

"Nicolas," she said. "Oh, Nicolas." And then she was pushing back against the crowd and struggling to force her grand skirt between the pressing bodies. Behind her, the Constable exchanged a worried glance with the ladies, who sighed and remarked that the burdens their poor friend endured took a toll upon her gentle soul. "Don't allow Sarah to leave alone," they scolded.

The Constable followed the widow, looking over his shoulder more often than not. He knew the black man's feet had just left the block as Sarah reached the carriage and he stepped forward to help her inside.

"I must return home at once," she said, cheeks red from exertion. She twisted the rich green fabric of her dress. Nicolas was awaking. Doctor Steenwycks, New York's most esteemed expert in matters of life and death, had admitted the possibility. And if not, if justice did not reach her son with its tender breath, she would cradle his head one last time in her arms and bury him in a manner befitting a king — scarves, gloves, mourning rings. She would spare no expense.

With a word from the Constable the carriage set forth. This time it stopped only once: in front of her house on Bridge Street.

Without waiting for the Constable to offer his supporting arm, Sarah raced to her front porch and threw open the door. Foul air tore through her like the clawed paws of a bear, and she bent before the sting of the assault. Nan looked up at her, small in the seat Sarah had pulled beside the settee.

"Can I go now, Missus?" Had she seen a ghost, Nan could not have looked more drawn.

"Fetch a candle," Sarah demanded. The Constable stood inside now, coughing, hands clenched against the instinct to cover his mouth and nose.

Nicolas would rise, or not. The waiting had ended.

"Untie the linens," Sarah said, stepping aside so the Constable could approach the settee. He paused a moment, regarding her with something akin to fear. "Come along now," she said.

"My dear — " the Constable began, but she silenced him with a wave.

"Must I call Doctor Steenwycks?" She moved to stand at the end of what she'd come to think of as Nicolas's sickbed and placed a hand beneath her son's head. Moisture had soaked the sheet and the cushion beneath it, leaving the fabric cold and damp.

The Constable, bent over the boy, ran his fingers between the swathing layers of cloth, watching his own hand move as if it were a rodent, something filthy. He located the triple fold Doctor Steenwycks had pinned shut and worked the metal from the cloth. "May I suggest — "

"I remain here," Sarah said. The cloth was not yet open, but already she knew that Nicolas had not recovered. She knew without confirmation that her son was no longer alive. She knew. The horrid Negro had taken her son away.

The Constable sighed, his will weak beside the widow's. He stepped back as he slipped the cloth from the boy, allowing the ends of the sheet to fall to the floor. Turning to Sarah, he watched her eyes widen. She pulled her hands from under Nicolas's head, wiping them on her dress as if she could rub all contact away. The boy's head fell back. His skin had discolored, grotesque as it was the day the midwife first held him aloft, mottled blue and still covered in blood. Sarah had taken the babe in her arms and life had emerged from his lips as a scream that echoed now only in her voice.

"The light," Nan said. She cupped her dark hand around the flame and extended the burning wick toward Sarah, toward Nicolas. The flesh of her palm glowed; its lines had a deep red hue. The flame flickered. Sarah took it from the girl.

"Leave me, Nan." Her voice was hardly more than a whisper. "Leave my house."

Nan's eyes narrowed. "Who will care for you?"

"You can't dismiss her," the Constable interrupted. "She's one of the good ones, your Nan."

"Gather your belongings," Sarah continued. "Take Nicolas's old case."

Nan bowed her head. Her dress, patterned with stains of gravy, wash water, and soot, hung loosely from her shoulders. Her kerchief had slipped back, revealing her high forehead. For a moment she waited, defiant. Then she ran from the room.

"You must not —" the Constable began. But Sarah did

not heed his words, her eyes on the fire, the delicate motion of flame.

"I have," she said. And the Constable had time just to take the candle from her and set it safely down before she collapsed into his arms, her face powdered and damp and, for the first time in her life, a perfect white.

❧ My Name Is Lubbert Das ❧

My name is Lubbert Das, and I was born with a stone in my head twenty-odd years ago. I never learned to read or make sums, I'm fat as a swollen wineskin, and before Father died and Doctor Theodorus Steenwycks discovered me, I chopped firewood from sunrise till midafternoon, when I had to pile the logs into cart seventeen, which pulled them to the barracks above the Common. At night Mother baked meat pies, or did till the money ran out and we started to burn furniture a few table legs at a time for heat. Now we eat hard bread on the floor, where we still have boards down, and pile our plates in a corner. No one has British pounds, except the people with horses and coaches, and not even they do sometimes.

Since Father died, Mother has worked for the milliner.

Her fingers are always yellow-brown and wrinkled no matter how hard she scrubs them. Her skin is as tough as her voice when she raises it so all the neighbors can hear her say that she and her dim-witted boy won't end up at the almshouse. There's disease at the almshouse, that's what they say, the soldiers up at the Common who always have money for hats. I've delivered six of them to as many officers' wives the past three months. The Sons of Liberty say the British are robbing us and we'll end up like African slaves if we don't change our ways, but the soldiers order more hats than anyone else in the colonies, and Mother says she needs to sell hats or we can't eat.

I don't chop wood for the soldiers anymore; the cart men won't take it. We refuse to supply the enslavers, they say. My ax, bright as the moon, sits in the corner, but I've started to steal what's left of the wood to burn at home because we don't have much but clothes left for our fires. I have my extra wool breeches and a few pairs of stockings; Mother, her summer clothes and Father's old broadcloth coat, which she wears around the house at night. It makes her cry, that faded blue coat, but she won't burn it. I tried to take it from her once so she'd feel better, and she hit me hard across my cheek, and then cried some more and begged God for forgiveness because I knew not what I did.

I wanted to go with Father the day he went to see the cocks fight, and I still thank God for his almighty kindness, because Father refused and I didn't die when men started drinking and fighting. Instead I met Doctor Theodorus Steenwycks, who came by our house in Church Farm along with the men carrying Father's body. The doctor brought a half tankard of ale, which Mother drank right there. Her face turned red, and she fell asleep just when the neighbors arrived to see what all the wailing was about. Miss Willett wrapped her arms around me, and I thought she might cry, too, but instead she started saying, "Poor dear. Poor dear. Whatever will he do now?"

I had to push her away because I was having unclean thoughts. Miss Willett has lived next door since I was a baby, and I remember her like a first snow, white and smothering. She used to give me hard candies and apples and sing me songs about the moon and King George of England. She always smiled when she saw me and hugged me close when I ran over to tell her about my day — I'd seen a fish in Fresh Water Pond; I'd watched the sailors arrive from faraway places with dark-skinned men and boxes that smelled as divine as baby Jesus himself.

Miss Willett released me when I pushed her back, and I saw that she did have tears in her eyes. I had to go outside then, because her sister tried to hold me as well, and that's when Doctor Steenwycks asked me if I knew my name. He was standing by the road, which was thick as porridge since the snow melted, his hands in his pockets, a small cocked hat on his head. He had red gums, fish-innards red, and I couldn't look at him for fear I might make an impolite expression or stare like Mother always forbids me to do. So I just nodded, big nods so he'd be sure to see.

"That's a good man," he said. "You're the man of the family now."

I nodded again and folded my hands behind my back like I'd seen the minister do.

"Can you speak?"

"Yes," I said.

"You understand me?"

He stepped closer, and I feared his opening mouth, but I knew Mother would want me to answer, so I turned my face away and nodded. He leaned closer and whispered, "I've cured men like you — even men so mad they can't dress themselves." Doctor Steenwycks was the son of a famous doctor. A doctor who cured the dead, Mother told me later, when I asked her about him.

"I dress myself," I said.

"Would you like to be cured? Would you like that?" Doctor Steenwycks smiled, red lips and gums. "You could care for your mother. Perhaps even find a wife. A good woman like — like a solid pair of bronze-buckled shoes."

I thought of Miss Willett with her long gray-brown braid. She had a brother who brought her paper-wrapped slabs of smoked bacon and dried beef, which she sometimes shared with Mother. She smelled like fresh leaves.

"How—" But I couldn't think of the words I needed to say because Miss Willett was there in my head, twirling like she might on Pope's Day, skirt flowing around her ankles, chest pressing against the tight fabric of her one good brown dress.

"There, there." Doctor Steenwycks placed a heavy hand on my shoulder. "It's not proper to be jumping up and down on the day of your poor father's death. But I'm a charitable man, a man who cannot stand by as fate's hideous hand reduces a good family, one already sorely burdened, to dire circumstance. We Steenwyckses believe in the common good; we help common folk. My father—you may know him, the great Jan Steenwycks—ah, but you wouldn't, of course you wouldn't. My father and I open our doors to people like you. Tell your mother to come by my parlor on Monday. Crown Street, near Trinity Church."

I repeated Doctor Steenwycks's words so I would not forget them before Mother awoke, which she did two hours later. Doctor Steenwycks and Miss Willett and her sister and all the men who'd arrived with the body had left by then along with Father's corpse. All that remained of the afternoon was a layer of mud and excrement on our floor.

"Dear Mother," I said, and she ran her fingers through

my hair and kissed my forehead and told me how blessed I was to be a fool. "Doctor Steenwycks says he can cure me."

THE GROUNDS IN FRONT of Doctor Steenwycks's house had eleven elm trees and seven white stone figures of unclad people. I touched one to see if it felt warm, but Mother pulled me away. The front porch was big as our house, and covered, and the doctor sat in one corner with a Negro girl. He was reading to her, and she was watching him, but she looked scared, crouched with her dress pulled tight over her knees. I was scared, too, but I followed Mother up two stairs to the porch and over to the corner where I saw that the man wasn't Doctor Steenwycks, but someone much older.

"Theodorus is in the back parlor," the man said. He smiled, like Doctor Steenwycks had, and I realized that he was the famous doctor, the one who cured the dead.

"I'm very pleased to meet you," Mother said, and she made a kind of curtsy. I told him my name was Lubbert, Lubbert Das. I was about to ask him to cure my father, when Mother took my shoulder and we walked through the front doors; there were two, and they opened in opposite directions from each other. We passed through four empty rooms with stone hearths and burning fires, till we found Doctor Steenwycks.

"You've arrived," he said. He'd been writing and his fingers were stained with black ink. He ran his hand over my head, and I thought he might stain my hair, which is brown but not dark, not like the stains on his hands.

"In France, the operation takes less than an hour. Here, with my tools, it will take somewhat longer." Doctor Steenwycks looked at Mother, who had borrowed a plumed hat from the milliner. He stared at her a very long time, so long her cheeks changed color.

"He's all I have," she said.

"We remove only a small portion of the skull, a fragment of bone. Once the pressure in his skull has lessened, the brain membrane will heal. He may — well, suffice it to say that he will be able to secure employment. And with the passage of time, he may one day become an intellectual. Once I've restored the proper flow of blood to his brain — "

"Your father taught you this . . . this cure?"

"My father has his specialty, I have mine. We are both great doctors, in our own way."

Mother nodded, and I could tell she was impressed but was trying to hide it, which is why she bit her lip and looked down. Doctor Steenwycks watched her, and I almost said yes because I knew that's what he wanted Mother to say and why he was waiting and I didn't want him to look at her any longer.

"I can't afford to pay you, not all at once," Mother said.

I sat down on the floor because Doctor Steenwycks's chairs reminded me of the ones the men were burning in the streets. Last time the Sons of Liberty marched through the streets, I tried to explain that the figures they held aloft were not really men, but bundles of straw that would never burn like people. Straw burns bright and quick, and once the fire fades, the black dust makes your insides dark and sore so that even breathing hurts. The Sons only swept me along to the docks, where they threatened to burn stamps in addition to their straw governors, and I thought about my ax and wished I'd brought it with me so that I could chop some of the dock posts down and bring them home to Mother.

"You drill a small hole in the skull," the doctor was saying, "an acorn-sized hole."

"Won't the bone shatter?"

"No, no."

Doctor Steenwycks's parlor had striped paper on the walls, and gold-framed mirrors hung on every side so that we appeared inside the walls: Mother in her mourning black and fancy hat, Doctor Steenwycks, and me, tremendous me, with my back to the others, peering into one mirror while trying to catch myself in another through the corner of one eye. I still believe that if I'd done it, seen myself in two places at one time, I would have disappeared. I would have joined my father in the place behind the glass, where

I'd be seen, as I saw my father, only in the thick lines of my nose or in the mossy brown color of my hair. Mother would have nothing if I disappeared. It was selfish of me to try.

"Next week," Mother said. "I can bring him next week."

Both Mother and Doctor Steenwycks stood, and in the mirror I could see them staring down at me. The room was large and the ceiling high, and for a moment I couldn't move. I'd remain forever in this one grand room of Doctor Steenwycks's grand house, which smelled sweet like honeysuckle and old like the docks.

"You take care of your mother now." Doctor Steenwycks extended an arm to help me rise, but when I turned from the mirror to take his hand, he'd moved it to the other side. He was backward, like everything since Father died and cart seventeen stopped arriving for my chopped kindling because the British were bad people. Perhaps the king's soldiers burned their furniture, too, though the only time I'd seen polished wood chairs in flames, the furniture had been stolen. If Mother and I had chairs like Doctor Steenwycks's, I think we would have preferred the cold to burning them.

I REMEMBER THE WEEK before my operation because everyone was angry. Miss Willett yelled at her sister because the milk had soured; her sister yelled back because she'd been robbed in the street and lost a dozen eggs and two pounds of butter; Mother complained that the neighbors had ceased to care for her and her plight; the Sons of Liberty rioted in front of the mayor's house; and the British hauled cannons from their ships to our streets, which they dragged to the walls of Fort George. Since I no longer worked, I walked down to look at the cannons — heavy, like me, only made of dark metal. I would have touched them, but as soon as I neared, the soldiers ordered me away.

The moon was growing smaller each night, and I was angry, too. I wanted to be cured. I lay on my sleeping mat and imagined Miss Willett. In her long brown dress she danced beside me, only this time, instead of patting my back, she kissed me as I've seen Mother and Father kiss. Miss Willett was there when I closed my eyes, when I opened them, when I woke, when I dreamed. Doctor Steenwycks had promised to make me a man Miss Willett might love, and when I saw her outside — hanging laundry or carrying an ordure tub to dump in the river at night — I stared. I saw her hips move and imagined the skin under homespun fabric. I imagined the undergarments I'd seen on her line. I watched her, and Mother saw me watching and told me I'd best go pray to God for forgiveness, and I was angry, but all I could do was drink a bowl of soap water hoping to cleanse my soul.

I spoke with her only once that week, as she was folding bed linens into the basket she'd used for as long as I remembered. Mother tells me I have no memory, that things change and I don't even notice, but I'm certain that Miss Willett's basket is the same one she brought over to our house the day I was born, filled with fresh apples she'd picked that weekend.

"How is your mother?" she said.

She was wearing black, too, and I thought she might be mourning Father, but she explained that her brother had died, that's why both she and her sister dressed in dark colors. He'd passed quietly in his sleep. Sixty-five to the day, she said, and healthy till he closed his eyes and began to dream. "It's dreams that kill us," she said. "And dreams that keep us alive."

I nodded, because I was pleased by her smile and couldn't think of anything beyond the line of her chin, which reminded me of a perfect log — rounded and firm.

Sunday, the minister spoke about loyalty — to our country, our God, and our king. I counted fifty-six women, fifty men, and three dozen children attending, along with seven odd persons: girls who had breasts, boys who had men's bodies, and one child who might be either boy or girl. I found the last most troublesome. When the minister asked us to dwell upon the things we held dear, I watched the boy-girl hoping it might become clear — or rather that it might be neither male nor female but something special, like dog or pig or cart horse. Mother cried, and I took her hand. When she prayed, she asked God to make me sane, to guide Father to heaven, and to give her strength in these dark times.

After church, she scolded me for staring. It wasn't proper for a man my age to be looking at children, especially girls.

"Lubbert," she said. "I need you to help me."

I reached for her hand, but she pulled it away and I saw she was trembling. The wind slapped us both, and I wished Father were there to put his arm around her. I stood straight as I could, though my shoulders rolled forward. I stared at the ground. Cobblestones passed, forty-seven, before we turned right and the streets became dirt again.

At our doorstep, Mother told me she prayed to God every day that I would get better. I nodded, though I was watching Miss Willett, who was tending to her Indian herbs. She'd explained them all to me many times, one for the stomach, one the head, one the throat. All of them had to do with health, though she told me she liked to flavor soup with cat's foot and roast meat with master wort.

Mother took some parsley, which she baked into johnny-cakes that night. We sat side by side on the floor and devoured them one at a time. We finished them all, even without Father's help.

MOTHER GAVE DOCTOR STEENWYCKS a sugar cake, and she wore a new hat—a bright blue one that

matched her eyes — the day she brought me to him. I knew
the way to the doctor's house and wanted to go alone, but
I had trouble explaining, as I always do, and so we went
together, she holding my hand. I'd washed my neck and
behind my ears, and my skin was still rough where bits of
soap adhered. I'd looked for Miss Willett before we left,
but she'd not yet risen, or had risen and already left.

Doctor Steenwycks greeted us at the front door. He held
a metal can in one hand, which he said he'd used to water
the flowers. I looked at all the flower beds across the front
porch, but I saw nothing blooming. Not the season for it,
but I didn't say anything. I didn't see the old doctor or the
Negro girl, but I looked for them, too.

The doctor smiled his horrible red smile and asked
Mother to wait in the sitting room while he performed the
operation. Mother refused, and so the three of us prepared
for my sanity. I sat in one of the chairs this time, Doctor
Steenwycks stood over me, and Mother knelt on the floor
by my side, her head bent in prayer. She had not removed
her hat, and it troubled me, a giant blue eye regarding me
without expression. Or perhaps it had expression, but I
didn't care for it: a spiral of blue wrapped in ribbon pulled
tightly.

"Beneath this surface is the cranial vault," the doctor
said. He'd shaved my hair with a straight razor and was
running his fingers over my head. I found them comforting,

warming. He had soft skin that smelled of lavender oils —
more like Mother's than Father's, though Mother never
wore perfume. "Do you want to feel?"

"No," Mother said. "Just remove the obstruction."

He showed me his surgical instrument — an obsidian
knife he promised could cut through my bones. Again I
thought of my ax, though I didn't care for the thought of
the doctor touching it. I watched him in the mirror on the
far wall. He looked bigger than me, though I outweighed
him by at least three stone, and he fussed over my scalp
just as the milliners fussed over wooden heads with felt and
tulle.

When Doctor Steenwycks cut through my skull, the
sound troubled me, the scrape of the knife on bone. It hurt,
but not as bad as the time I sliced open my thumb chop-
ping wood. Mother cried out at the blood, which stained
her hat badly enough that she could never return it. I'd delivered one very like it to an officer's wife, and I was thinking that perhaps I could return to the barracks and steal it
when Doctor Steenwycks declared the operation a success.
He recommended bed rest and sent us home after kissing
Mother's left hand.

"How do you feel?" Mother asked when we reached the
street.

I nodded because I felt much as I had that morning, only
cooler, exposed, and a little dizzy. My skin stung where the

doctor had cut it, and I thought I might fall down and that everything was moving extremely rapidly: the sea gulls, the people, and street carts. I wished for a hat, as I'd forgotten to bring one, and in the excitement of the morning not even Mother had noticed.

A pair of man-boys were walking toward us with their arms raised in fists. "We've won! We've won!" they called.

I wondered how they knew of my appointment and how, without asking, they guessed I'd been cured.

The man-boys were abreast of us now, and I recognized them from the day on the docks, and I believe they recognized me, too, because they smiled and spoke to me — not Mother, which is what people usually do: King George repealed the stamp tax. We are free. Somewhere nearby, a musket fired, and the man-boys cheered again and wished us well.

"That's wonderful news," Mother said. "Truly wonderful. Hat sales have been so low, and no one wants imported satin or, well, anything fashionable."

I wondered if cart seventeen would come for my firewood again, though it was nearly April and soon New York would be so hot that no one — not even British soldiers — would want heating fires.

"I feel — " I began again, and Mother grabbed my hand. She'd forgotten the blood on her hat, which had darkened to a brownish color.

"Oh, what a glorious day. What a glorious, glorious day," she said.

I'VE HAD A HOLE in my head for nearly three months now. The skin has healed, but not grown smooth. Miss Willett likes to run her finger over the opening, which is as big as the tip of her pinky. She says it's wonderful to be so close to a human brain. And she marvels that I've been saved. She says "saved," not "cured," though I've always gone to church and said my prayers before bed. I brought her a bouquet of purple irises I found growing in Bowling Green. I go there after work sometimes to look for the statue of King George that the Common Council promised after the stamp tax was repealed. The king must be large, like me, only made of dark metal. The flowers would look pretty beside his foot. I thought of Miss Willett, and she smiled when I handed her the stems.

"No one's brought me flowers in years," she said. I waited for her to kiss me like I imagined she would, but she never leaned forward. Instead she turned to her sister, who was helping her hang clothes, and they laughed.

I wanted to tell her that she was beautiful, that I'd loved her since the day I was born, that I remembered her face as it was then, because of the stone in my head. I know it was the stone that held her image, because now that it is gone, I can't quite remember whether her dress was brown or gray that day, or whether she carried apples in her laundry basket or in the metal can in which she stores extra soil.

"I love you," I said, and she patted my back and told me I was cured and shouldn't waste time with old women like her. I could start a family, a business. I pulled her close to me, but she still did not kiss me, and though I tried to find her lips with mine, she turned her face so that I tasted only hair. I never planned to let her go, but the constable arrived and I heard screaming and now I may not speak to Miss Willett or the law will take me away.

I work with Mother at the millinery now, delivering hats and crates of fabric from the docks. The milliners say I'm good-natured, that I look like my Mother, that I have a kind and generous heart. Mother seems happier. She's hung Father's broadcloth coat on a peg, and now that it is warmer, she never wears it. Only I take it down from the wall. The coat is far too small for me. But I want to remember it as it is.

Doctor Steenwycks calls on us every few days, even when I'm not home. I have nightmares about him, and I think he loves Mother, and when I tell her, she laughs and tells me I know nothing of love. But I have a hole in my head, where Doctor Steenwycks removed my stone. And I know I have been cured.

Hysteria

Dressed in a top hat and shadbelly coat of broadcloth, Doctor Willis Steenwycks carried a whip, though he never once struck his mare with it. The cool air bestowed a healthy glow to his skin, and even as he gazed absently ahead he appeared content. Only his wife, Elizabeth, and his closest friends at the philological society would note his wrinkled brow and know him to be preoccupied. He had, in fact, been troubled all morning by his headstrong daughter, Edith.

The girl, a comely brown-haired child with her mother's eyes and narrow shoulders, was practically a woman. She'd completed her schooling: she spoke French and played piano — Mozart and Bach, as well as the latest sonatas by Dussek; she wrote sums as well as the doctor could; she was well versed in the natural sciences and had much of the first book of the *Scientific Dialogues* committed to memory; she tutored her six-year-old brother — a slight, pale boy who tended to sleep under his bed where no one could see him — and helped him tie laces and fasten buttons. She'd been taught grace and good posture; she knew how to receive men and how to flatter them. Yet she took no suitor, despite numerous offers. Instead she spent her days at Newgate Prison helping George Stuart, a queer Quaker reformer, "improve the prisoners' condition."

Doctor Steenwycks was, he admitted, partially to blame. Ever since George Washington and the capital moved away from New York to Philadelphia, then to Washington, D.C., he'd felt such a dearth of intellectualism that he encouraged his daughter to seek out what few thoughtful men remained. As much as the doctor mistrusted George Stuart's radical ideas about reform, the man was well connected. With him came possibilities, potential mates, mates other than Edmund, the banker whom Elizabeth had handpicked for the girl. The boy was earnest enough, but his mind was as soft as the line of his chin. Modern women should have choice, and the doctor hoped that his daughter would find her own well-bred young man and leave good works to the less fortunate, who required such pastimes in lieu of fine dining. He didn't want his daughter to settle for anything less than she desired. He didn't want her to reach his age and begin to wonder, What if I had married someone else?

What if the perfect lover still waits for me, only I gave in too soon? What if happiness, perfect wedded bliss, exists? What if . . . And so he let the girl continue her work and let his wife's hard stares wash over him — at least until last night, the girl's sixteenth birthday.

"She said she won't ever marry, not when so many poor souls need her so much more," Elizabeth sobbed as the doctor stroked her hair. The sixteen years of their marriage had taught him that outbursts such as these required immediate attention, and his evening brandy languished on the bedside table beside a smoke-blackened lamp and a slice of sweet currant bread. Elizabeth hated crumbs, particularly in the bedclothes, but Doctor Steenwycks enjoyed a late-evening repast and, with some trepidation, did on occasion defy his wife's wishes. The house was his, after all: 62 Orchard Street, an establishment three stories tall, with four chimneys and both a front and rear porch. His father had built it after Willis's half brother, Lubbert, died in the war fires that burned down the old residence on Crown Street. Best to start over, he'd said, and he purchased a substantial stretch of the old Delancy farm. From their new back parlor, first Theodorus and then Willis himself provided the best medical care in New York. Framed letters from four senators, mayor's wives, and world-renowned academics, dating as far back as 1718, attested to the family talent. Doctor Willis Steenwycks's fees, which Elizabeth collected and transformed into flocked wallpaper or a Turkish carpet or a string of pearls, were the highest in all of New York.

"I'll speak with her," he said.

"You'll speak with her at once." Elizabeth pulled away, her face red and puffy. "I won't have her going to that horrid prison. Enough! She'll be a penniless old maid, like my poor dear sister."

"No, no," the doctor said. Elizabeth's sister, who lived on nothing but fish heads and sour milk — or at least so it seemed by her smell — would have nothing to do with his lovely daughter. Still, he said nothing to Edith the next morning, even when the girl stood before him coaxing her young brother from the corner of the china cabinet, where he was attempting to hide a handful of feathers, not a dead bird, the doctor decided, though he detected what appeared to be a pronged foot and the curve of a wing. The doctor waved good-bye when Edith donned her hat and set out on foot for the prison. Not until Elizabeth threatened to go to the prison herself did he agree to fetch the child.

"It's for her own good," Elizabeth said, and the words still echoed in his head as he reigned in Tulip and turned onto Amos Street toward the imposing walled structure that stood on the river's shore. He would have a few words with George Stuart and then see to it that Edith returned home. Her days at the prison had come to a close.

Newgate Prison, which had opened its imposing arched wooden doors nearly twenty-four years earlier, rose like a fortress at the edge of New York, complete with a single domed turret and thick stone wall. The main gate was shut fast when Doctor Steenwycks arrived, and he had to tie his horse and wait for the sentry to guide him inside.

The warden's office was little more than a cell, the doctor noted as he introduced himself to George Stuart, a small, gray-haired man in dark trousers and an ill-fitting jacket — a man doomed, by appearance alone, to work with society's outcasts. How the warden had managed to gain so much influence troubled the doctor, in the way that magic tricks did, or a passion for music, or his son's tendency to spend long hours beneath the pantry shelves — all things beyond his comprehension.

"A pleasure," George said. "Your daughter tells me you're a medical man. Please sit down."

The doctor sat in the room's one chair, the cane seat worn nearly through, likely by George himself, who dragged the piece from the far side of his desk so that his guest could rest more comfortably. George leaned on the desktop and waited for the doctor to announce his purpose.

"A fine day," Doctor Steenwycks said, reluctant to express his concerns immediately. George Stuart was well respected and not a man to cross lightly. Single-handedly he had convinced the state legislature to fund prison reforms, and people whispered that he had connections to the governor and even the president. Besides, the message the doctor carried in truth belonged to Elizabeth, and the words felt heavy on his tongue.

"I have yet to go outside," George said.

The doctor nodded. Generous men, those devoted to selfless causes, made him uneasy, and he could think of no other small talk. "I've come about my daughter."

"A fine girl," George said. "Very kind and capable."

The doctor prided himself on his role in his daughter's upbringing. It was he who had found Mrs. Isabella Graham's Academy for Women and he who sat with his daughter as she learned arithmetic and logic. Years ago he'd hoped his firstborn would be a boy, but now that he had both a daughter and son, he realized that he much preferred to dwell on Edith, who required his guidance.

"It's time Edith marries," the doctor said.

"She'd make any man a fine wife."

"Very true. But she'll never find a husband among your prisoners."

"Once a man's been rehabilitated —"

"My daughter will not marry a murderer."

"We have only arsonists and burglars here," George said.

His eyes were the blue-gray of lichen or mold, and he didn't smile. Did he truly believe his prisoners suitors?

Doctor Steenwycks shook his head. "She leaves today."

"Would you like to collect her yourself?" He led the doctor through the narrow stone hallways lit dimly by the pale daylight.

The doctor never imagined the prison to be so large, nor that so many criminals had been apprehended. French Negroes, held four to a cell, stared at him with no sign of the remorse rehabilitation promised. Swarthy men in filth-covered work suits cussed, dirty fingers wrapped around iron bars. The air hung rank with decomposing straw and mildew.

"Not a place for a woman," he said.

"The women are in separate quarters." George smiled. "They have a separate recreational area as well. It's time for the afternoon exercises."

George unlatched a heavy wooden door and stepped aside so that the doctor could better view the small stone-walled courtyard. Packed dirt with matted brown clumps of dead grasses stretched beneath the bare feet of nearly two dozen women dressed in poorly fitted gowns that dragged along the ground on the shorter prisoners and barely covered the knees of the tallest — a redhead, with only one good eye and a mouthful of blackened teeth. She frightened even the doctor, who stood safely above her on an observation deck.

"She's new," George explained. "Got here yesterday. Stealing sweets."

The redhead gazed up at the men and laughed.

"When she first arrived, she was raving, tearing at her skin. But Edith spoke to her. Your girl works magic. Another week and even this madwoman will be healed."

The redhead had both hands on her breasts and was leering up at them. Her nails sank into the fabric of her dress, which she ripped open. Pale and bared, her breasts inspired the other women, who began to pull at their clothes as well. Hysterical, all of them — or worse, downright mad. One condition invariably led to the other, or at least so Doctor Steenwycks believed. He'd seen hysterical women on the streets — women so mad they'd forgotten language — and he had to walk briskly in order to avoid them. Just the week before, a young mother, her unfortunate babe pressed tight to a naked breast, had run after him, demanding small change and a crust of bread. The impropriety shocked him even now.

"Stop! Stop that right now."

Doctor Steenwycks turned at the familiar voice. Edith, dark hair pulled away from her face in a loose bun, was among the prisoners. She had a confidence he had never noted before, and he wasn't sure the change suited her. She looked too mature, less like a girl and more like a spinster.

"Come with me," Edith said. She placed a hand on the madwoman's forehead, stroked her hair. Silence fell over the courtyard.

"Edith!" the doctor called, but the prisoner, two feet taller and far broader in the shoulders than his daughter, had already accepted the girl's hand. The two strode together toward the courtyard door.

"Yes, your daughter has a way with prisoners," George said, his tone softening, his thin lips nearly forming a smile. "Even the most desperate and depraved — particularly those — respond to her. Respect her. Come, we can meet her by the cells."

Had he known the nature of his daughter's service, Doctor Willis Steenwycks would have come for her long before. He'd imagined that she read to the prisoners or taught them the Bible — tasks she could perform while the criminals remained behind bars.

"We have fifty-four eight-person cells here," George explained as he led the doctor down a short flight of stairs and through two more passageways, "and well over five hundred inmates — the largest rehabilitation facility in New York." He selected a key from his ring and unlocked an iron-braced door. "Your daughter —"

"Edith," the doctor said, more firmly now that the girl stood before him, beyond the threshold and so close he could reach forward and nearly touch her. Behind her, the redheaded woman pressed her face against the barred cell window. "Your mother and I —"

"Father! It's so kind of you to visit. You've met Mr. Stuart, I see."

"Yes." The doctor endured his daughter's embrace, certain she would not respond as fondly to the words he must now share. "Your mother and I need you to come home."

"Is everything all right?" Concern crossed the girl's face, and she stepped back.

"Your mother is very upset." Doctor Steenwycks reached out and took the girl's hand.

"I'll come home right after work. I promise."

"Edith." The doctor pulled the girl to his side. "You don't understand."

"If I leave, there'll be no one to help them." She turned to George, her eyes soft with a plea for his confirmation. When George said nothing, she frowned. "I suppose just this once — if it's truly important."

"I'll stay later tomorrow," she promised George, who looked past her to a mess of thrown porridge on the dusty prison floor.

"Your father —" George began.

"Your mother," Doctor Steenwycks interrupted. "Your mother and I have decided that your time here is done."

The meaning of her father's visit had at last sounded, and the doctor could feel his daughter's understanding in the muscles that tensed beneath her dress.

"This is my work, my calling," she said.

She struggled, attempting to free herself from his restraining arm.

"Edith, darling, you're hardly acting a lady." The doctor smiled at George, though the warden did not return the pleasantry. "You are a role model, a young lady. Come now, let's go home."

WHEN THE DOCTOR led Edith into the front parlor of 62 Orchard Street, the house smelled of butter. The cook had baked sugar cookies, a rarity reserved for special occasions. The fire was lit and the harpsichord stood open, bared keys inviting Edith to play. On most afternoons, the instrument remained closed and silent. A watercolor landscape for which the girl had won a blue ribbon hung on the wall, where it clashed with the red and gold wallpaper. For years the picture had remained in the bedroom cabinet for precisely this reason. Elizabeth, who usually retired for a nap in the early afternoon, sat on the couch, one arm wrapped around her young son. She'd been picking lice from the boy's scalp, or at least she had a cross expression, which the doctor attributed to contemplation of the minute and irritating. She extended an arm in greeting. "How nice of you to join us."

"I have a headache," Edith complained.

"From the prison, no doubt," Elizabeth said and, after her daughter turned her back and headed to her room, added, "She is only moping."

The doctor sat beside his wife and son and chewed a sugar cookie, which tasted no sweeter than gruel. His girl was resilient. She would recover her good spirits without his help.

Still, he slept poorly that night — his sleep torn with nightmare — and he woke before dawn to an overcast sky and a dampness that ached in his joints.

He was surprised when Edith, dressed neatly in a mustard dress, joined him for an early breakfast. He'd hoped to see her looking well, but he hadn't anticipated the bounce in her step or the cheerfulness in her voice when she said, "Good morning, Father."

She poured herself coffee with sugar and cream and drew up a chair beside him.

"You look lovely," he said.

"Thank you." She smiled and looked down, almost flirting. "I thought I'd go for a stroll this morning."

"It's going to rain," he said.

"If I left now — " Edith sipped her coffee, set down the cup, frowned. "Mother must need something from the market."

Willis Steenwycks was a doctor and a businessman. He could sense a lie as fast as his tongue recognized whiskey. "You aren't going back to that prison," he said.

"I," Edith began. "You can't — "

From the doorway, still dressed in her nightgown, Elizabeth interjected, "As long as you live in my house, you'll do as I say."

"You might be a bit more gentle," the doctor said to his wife. "She's — "

"We've been far too gentle for far too long."

The doctor nodded, the way he often did at work, when clients spoke of stomach pains or swollen joints and he only half listened. He could spend hours in conversation and remember very little, a habit he relied upon to carry him through till evening when he could retire to the dining room and the comfort of dinner and a few stiff drinks.

However, that night's dinner brought no pleasure. At six o'clock Edith refused to emerge from her bedroom. While the doctor and his son ate freshly baked meat pie, and Elizabeth, complaining of an upset stomach, nibbled on yesterday's sugar cookies, Edith stubbornly proclaimed her independence: "You can't order me to eat," or "You can't order me to listen" or, when her voice grew tired, simply screeching periodically to disrupt the meal.

"Headstrong," Elizabeth sighed.

At last the girl tired, for she remained silent when the knock came at the front door. The doctor set down his ale and rose to greet the newcomer. From behind the coatrack, his son peered up at him, wide, mischievous blue eyes reminding the doctor that the boy had left the table without excusing himself and ought to be sent away to school to learn discipline.

The night air was chilly and damp. Pressed close to the wall so the eave would shelter him from the drizzle, George Stuart stood on the doorstep, the scent of the prison still rough on him. He looked even smaller than he had the day before, and oddly threatening.

"I've come for Edith," George said. "She left this at Newgate."

From beneath his jacket, he produced a damp copy of Mary Wollstonecraft's memoirs, which he presented almost as if it were a great gift. From between the pages, the top of a neatly penned note protruded. "Dearest Edith," it began, though the doctor could not read further without betraying his interest.

"She's sleeping," the doctor said. "Quite exhausted, poor child."

"Will you tell her I called?"

A gracious man would have invited the warden inside. But Doctor Steenwycks did not want to wake his daughter, and he was certain that George Stuart's presence would anger his wife, who'd already blamed the evening's outburst on Newgate Prison.

"I'm sure she'll be delighted," he said. He closed the door behind the warden and returned to the table, where Elizabeth examined the book and proclaimed it rubbish.

"She must not learn that he called," she decided. "Having too many men around — particularly unsuitable ones — can bring only trouble." Elizabeth nodded knowingly.

Doctor Steenwycks gazed at his wife's nose to avoid her glare. Her skin was as rosy as it was the day he first met her at the seaside retreat, where she cleaned laundry and he vacationed. He'd loved another woman at the time, a curly haired girl named Madeline whom he courted daily with passionate letters. He sent flowers and candies, tried his hand at poetry, proposed numerous strolls. He even turned to Elizabeth for advice, took her into his confidence one afternoon when she appeared to collect his linens. She replied with the sense he grew to rely upon: a good marriage is built on mutual sympathy, companionship, and trust, not transient passion or base desire. How quickly she convinced him with her sound judgment and tongue to change the object of his desire — much too quickly he soon realized, but by then it was too late.

"We discussed Wollstonecraft at my philological society," he said curtly, and turned to fill his cup yet again. "I find her work quite compelling."

+ + +

Three nights passed, and for three nights Doctor Steenwycks felt as weightless as a falling leaf, blown forward and back between the wills of Elizabeth and Edith. He saw no good solution. He failed to sleep at night, and morning light made his thoughts no clearer.

"Willis," Elizabeth said to him, her hair still mussed from her pillow, "I think she needs a doctor."

He fastened a dressing gown over his nightshirt and poured a long measure of water into the porcelain washbowl. Edith had drawn him from his bed no less than five times last night, and the memory of her screamed demands — "Let me work!", "I am suffocating," and once, a foul word he could not bear to repeat — still ached in his head.

"I'd hoped it would pass," he said.

"She hasn't eaten in days." Elizabeth combed her hair, pulling out tangles without so much as a glance to the mirror. "I'm afraid it's more than willfulness. She's hysterical."

The girl had always been headstrong — insisting on joining her father when he entertained colleagues in the back parlor, or thrusting her opinions of England and monarchy upon those who still felt fondness for the king — but she'd also always had a healthy appetite.

"I'll examine her tomorrow."

"I think you should see her now. Even Edmund is concerned. He came calling and I had to send him away, poor lovesick boy. He's more alarmed than the girl's own father."

Again the doctor nodded, resigned. "I'll see to it right away."

Elizabeth led her husband to Edith's bedside and pointed at the girl as if Doctor Steenwycks could not recognize his own daughter. Pale and listless, the child looked so delicate that he could not resist the impulse to bend and stroke her hand. He stepped forward, knocking into the bed frame. The lace blanket Edith's aunt had knit slipped off the bed, revealing several volumes of political philosophy taken from his study. Elizabeth shook her head.

"How are you feeling?" he asked. His father had sent him abroad to study at the finest institutions, yet Willis never felt comfortable diagnosing his wife and children. He preferred to believe that his proximity alone prevented disease, that his family was immune to the complaints common patients brought.

Edith ignored her father as he bent to listen to her heartbeat and brush the hair back from her forehead to feel for warmth. She refused the water he offered, and she did not protest when Elizabeth took the books from the bed.

"Let me see your wrist," the doctor said, and she shook her head. When he grabbed her hand and pulled it toward the light, she murmured softly that she needed air. He pulled a jar of smelling salts from the bag he usually kept in the parlor.

"She's quite ill," Elizabeth determined. "Hysteria. Poor

child. I know it. She's forgotten most of her English no doubt."

"She was fine last week," the doctor said, almost defensively.

"I believe she's been self-polluting."

"Of course not!" Doctor Steenwycks began to redden. The uterus was such a troublesome organ, and false stimulation — especially after childbearing age — could cause the womb to wander. "She knows better than to — "

"A girl like Edith must have suitors."

"She's in no condition to receive suitors," Doctor Steenwycks said, impropriety's blush still hot in his cheeks.

"You must help her receive them then." Elizabeth took the smelling salts from her husband and waved them beneath Edith's nostrils. The sharp scent of ammonia and peppermint filled the air. "These should revive her long enough to meet gentlemen friends."

The doctor watched his unresponsive daughter. His role in her illness loomed dark in his thought. Elizabeth had been right, though it pained him to admit it. He should have intervened long ago, insisted that the girl heed her mother, find a husband, settle down. But how could he have known? He had no womb of his own, no uterine furies.

"It's good you *finally* went to her," Elizabeth said. "It's not too late — if *I* manage it — to find a husband."

DOCTOR STEENWYCKS CARRIED Edith to the parlor and laid her gently into the armed rocking chair while Elizabeth straightened the girl's dress and fussed with her hairpins. Her young brother watched from beneath the sideboard, his face smeared with jam.

Aside from her pallor and the dark circles beneath her eyes, Edith looked lovely. With her gaze unfocused, she had a new softness, an almost ethereal beauty, much like that of a curly haired girl the doctor had fancied years before. Gently he kissed his daughter's forehead.

He turned to light the chandelier, stoked the fire, poured himself a generous cup of brandy. Elizabeth had already set out the gilt-edged china and a tea tray with biscuits, preserves, and fresh cream. The carpet had been swept, the looking glass dusted, the andirons, shovel, and tongs arranged neatly. Between his daughter and the slat-bottomed chair set out for her suitor, a pot of black tea steeped.

"That must be Edmund," Elizabeth said, responding to the knock at the front door.

The doctor retreated to his alcove, where a card table served as a makeshift writing desk. He'd set the table up there so he could chaperon Edmund's visit, though he did not imagine the young man would misbehave. He was a reasonable man, steady and reliably dull.

Willis was tired, exceedingly so. He'd slept scarcely three

hours since he'd taken Edith home — an insomnia he at first blamed on his daughter's outbursts, though last night she'd slept silently, while he wandered through the darkened house alone. Twice he was certain he'd seen ghosts: faint glows, unexpected motion around his armchair and near the unswept hearth of his son's bedroom. On closer examination he found nothing, confirming the ravings of his sleepless thought.

Still, he had business to attend to — piling receipts and unsigned bills — and a small personal matter: a response to a letter from a recent widow, which he'd kept folded in his pocket since it arrived two weeks earlier, smelling of old lavender.

"Good day, Mr. Steenwycks," Edmund said. Fear for his beloved's health had not stolen the suitor's appetite, and he looked, if anything, plumper than he had the last time the doctor had seen him. He wore a striped velvet coat with a muslin cravat and white dress shirt, and no trousers, though when the doctor looked closer, he realized that his eyes were playing tricks on him again. Cream-colored trousers stretched tightly around the boy's middle.

"My stomach is alive with nervous energy," Edmund proclaimed, spreading a thick layer of jam over the quick bread Elizabeth offered.

"She's been anxious to see you," she said. "I'm so glad you could come."

The doctor watched for signs of recognition in his daughter's face. He'd administered the smelling salts as prescribed, but Edith only coughed violently and glared. Now she gazed to the wall behind Edmund's shoulder.

"I'll leave you." Elizabeth smiled and turned toward the kitchen.

Edmund finished his biscuit and reached for another. "Dearest — " he began. "Darling. I've missed you, and your condition is . . . well, your mother's explained. I . . . it matters not to me. I care for you now, just as I — "

"I despise you," Edith said.

Perturbed by the venom in his daughter's voice, the doctor set down his pen, drained his cup, and poured himself another brandy.

"I know you are ill, that it's disease speaking through gentle lips," Edmund said.

"Leave," Edith said.

"You mustn't allow passion to interfere with your health." Edmund stepped forward and bent down to adjust Edith's blanket. "I've come here to help you."

"I know why you've come. They tell me I've lost my reason, that I'm sick. But I know better."

Doctor Steenwycks watched, distressed by his daughter's sudden outburst. She had not spoken coherently in days. Perhaps, he decided, her womb sensed Edmund's presence.

"If you truly loved me, you'd leave now," Edith said.

"Who else would take you?"

"Father!" Edith called, though it was Elizabeth who came running.

"She doesn't mean it," Elizabeth said.

"Perhaps I should call again, when she's feeling more receptive." Edmund dabbed the jam from his chin.

"He's our only hope," Elizabeth cried, and the doctor realized his wife now addressed him.

"I —" he began.

"I won't have him." Edith tore the bronze pin from her hair. "Tell them, Father."

"You will," Elizabeth said, "if I have to lock myself in my room and starve till you take him — how would you like that, your own mother driven to madness?"

"Elizabeth," Doctor Steenwycks rose. For the past few nights, fatigue had prevented him from satisfying his wife's appetites, and he worried that she, too, might now suffer hysteria's effects. He considered the red and blue weave of the carpet. When his daughter married, she would stand on this very rug, just as he had stood beside Elizabeth in her parents' parlor sixteen years before. Elizabeth had looked matronly then in her full brown gown and silver necklaces. She'd promised him guidance and support; he'd promised her comfort and faithfulness. Many marriages survived on less. Perhaps Edith would learn to care for Edmund.

Perhaps she would find health and happiness. He tried to picture his girl, his lovely daughter, beside a man he knew she loathed. If she had an affair, took another lover — later, once she'd regained her health — he'd turn a blind eye. That much he could do, he decided, as the warm glow of brandy made it increasingly clear that some marriages were meant to be broadened.

He did not hear the knock at the front door, only Elizabeth's order that he receive the guest. Didn't she realize that Edmund stood before her, drawing inferences about married life? Didn't she sense that she, not Edith, might frighten the young man away with her sharp, incessant demands? The doctor sipped, swallowed, decided to take a quick stroll and allow the fresh air to soothe his brandy dizziness.

At the door, a wild-eyed man stood with a half-dozen unkempt companions. They wore faded trousers and spent shoes. "Since Edith won't come to the prison, we've come to visit her instead — to thank her for our rehabilitation," the wild man said.

"I'm afraid — " the doctor began.

"We'd like to thank her for all she's done for us," a second man offered through a mouthful of chipped and missing teeth. "We were released today."

For a moment the doctor considered. How would his wife react to the bearded man with the scar etched deep in the flesh of his lip? Or the lice-ridden fellow in the stained blue shirt? He stepped aside. "Come in," he said as the men filed past him. "Turn left to the parlor."

"What is this?" he heard Elizabeth demand. "Who are these men?"

The doctor lingered at the doorway, pondering love and contentment. Or love and joy. Or maybe not love at all, but loathing and compromise.

"Get out of my home!" Elizabeth shrieked. A table crashed against the floor amidst a clatter of breaking china.

The doctor stepped away from the door and into the street. The sky threatened rain. But the brandy brought confidence. He wouldn't just stroll, he'd leave. He was leaving. He had the address in his pocket, the soft-scented note penned in the hand of his old beloved. Scandal, what scandal there was, would trouble Elizabeth more than his absence.

"One should not decide rashly; one should not allow passion to rule," he muttered. Elizabeth's words, not his. Not anymore, though the thought of his wife brought a heaviness to his head. He felt dizzy. He drew a quick breath. His feet moved beneath him without touching the ground. He was stumbling, falling. The cool, damp street caught him, comforted him. He looked up.

He was facing his doorway, he realized. He'd gotten turned around, or the world had spun. But it didn't matter.

A sudden joy pulled him back to his feet; he stood, trans-fixed. For there, in front of his house, and not a day aged, stood Madeline, his Madeline. She held a wrapped par-cel — clothing most likely — and a leather bag containing her savings. She wavered unsteadily, her gaze upon him, an apparition pulled from the tumulus depths of his dreams.

"You've come to me," he said, reaching out. "You've come just as I was on my way."

"I love you," he said, and added, when the girl remained silent, "Can you forgive me? Can you ever forgive me?"

And then she was in his arms, delicate, sobbing, grateful for his words, he believed, and he pressed his lips against the top of her head.

"Darling, darling," he whispered. "Madeline, my Made-line, my darling Madeline." He reached for the wall to steady himself, but his hand met only the air. He was in the street, he remembered, the street in front of his home.

The girl pulled back and regarded him, her brows bent with concern. "Come with me," she said at last. The warmth of her hand on his forehead brought comfort and peace. He followed her, his steps unsteady, toward his house, their house. Already he knew she was not Madeline. Already he knew he'd been foolish and tired, so tired and drunk. But she had a great gift, this girl of his — a kindness he could not, would never, escape. And for the first time in days, the doctor believed that everything was about to get better.

Reading Grandpa's Head

The night Morris's first letter arrived, Edith returned home late from the Institute. She draped her shawl over Grandpa's favorite chair, set her notebooks on the end table, and announced her arrival with the single dry cough she'd perfected over her thirty-three years. Had she simply said, "I've returned," Grandpa would not have responded. Her voice would have faded to silence, as it often did when she relayed facts her father knew or would rather not hear spoken.

Grandpa, knit cap pulled tight over his forehead, emerged from his study. Despite his age, he cured people seven days a week, going door to door with his frock coat pockets full of scissors, metal syringes, lancets, glass bleeding cups, and a handful of licorice suckers.

"It's time for you and Letty to make other arrangements," he said, his tone level and the words evenly spaced. He had clearly practiced the line all day.

"Oh, Father," Edith said.

She and Letty had just moved in to 62 Orchard Street. Not six months had passed since her husband, Morris, set out for the territories leaving Edith and Letty at Grandpa's doorstep with a promise to call for them soon.

Letty emerged from the kitchen and stepped forward to hug her mother. At thirteen, she stood as tall as Edith, and she could reach and sweep clean the high shelves where Grandpa hid flasks of foul-smelling brandy. Days, while he made his rounds, she pored over his medical texts, convinced that to be truly moderate, one must eat only fresh fruits and boiled vegetables. She was as strong-willed as Edith had been, long ago, before the strain of illness and cooking and cleaning and caring for three children, two of whom had died in infancy, had dulled her passions.

"Mother, I ruined Grandpa's good shirt," she said. The fire had nearly expired beneath her watch, and the plates from yesterday's supper still sat on the table. "It caught on the washboard."

In days past, Edith would have scolded her daughter, admonished her to exert more care. But now she dismissed the words with a wave. She'd known of her daughter's inattentiveness for weeks, ever since Letty sat beneath Edith's inquiring fingers and she examined the bumps and sutures of the girl's head. "I read that all in your skull," she said.

"Really, Edith," Grandpa said. "You can't predict what a person will do by the shape of his head."

Edith stepped past Grandpa to the fire, which she fed so ineptly that it diminished further. The wallpaper, discolored in places where lamp oil had splattered, peeled around the trim. Hard times had come to New York, and Grandpa had let go the hired help — an old woman and her son — who, Edith suspected, had done little more than steal from her father.

"You should come with me," she said. "The demonstrations are breathtaking."

"No respectable doctor —"

"Doctor Ketchum was there."

Grandpa folded his arms over his plain black waistcoat. His eyes followed Edith's hands as she removed her gloves, now tinged gray with ash, and dropped them on top of his seat cushion.

"Edith —" he began, but Letty interrupted, pointing at Grandpa accusingly.

"You've been smoking." She peered around him to his study off the back parlor. She'd thrown away a tin of his horrid weed last Saturday, but the old man must have another hiding place. Perhaps he'd pulled forward *Experiments and Observations on the Gastric Juices* again, stashing the tin behind the well-worn pages, or the *Gazetteer of England*, for which he had absolutely no other use.

"Clear the table," Grandpa ordered, but Letty was already searching for the tobacco.

Edith sighed. Gone were the quiet evenings when her mother managed the house while Grandpa discussed news and medicine with his son — a vain, foolish child who'd run off with the circus years before. Now Edith had to attend to the household; she could not retire, as her heart urged, to review her lecture notes.

EARLIER THAT DAY Edith's mentor, Fowler Corender, had examined a pauper, a frail alcoholic known for falling dead asleep along the Bowery. "Behold!" Fowler cried as he shaved the poor man's scalp with a flat razor and ran his bare fingers over the pale, nubby skin. "A rather small covetiveness organ, and a large appetite. Is it no wonder the man drinks? And note the prominent protuberance here on the parietal bone. This man was born to live in the streets."

A smattering of applause, led by Edith, brought a glow to Fowler's cheeks. Though he claimed to prefer silence and solitude, he performed public demonstrations three afternoons a week and had considered adding an evening show. Plastered on the wall behind him, a chart demarcated the thirty-three brain organs Doctor Spurzheim had catalogued, as well as the six dozen facilities he, Fowler, had discovered while working in New York. The chart served as a reference for those new to the sessions; Edith no longer referred to it.

As young Fowler's apprentice, she took careful notes while he called out observations. Only yesterday, he'd discovered a new organ: solicitousness, which resided in the superior anterior region of the skull and had thus far eluded scientific discovery, he maintained, because of its almost imperceptible size. Of all the eminent scientists, Fowler Corender had the most sensitive fingers, an asset he boasted about often. He removed his jacket when he worked, revealing embroidered suspenders and a single-breasted vest. His feet were small, and looked even more so in pointy shoes. He'd studied abroad, in Edinburgh, where he worked with the finest minds of the century. He'd even met Spurzheim, by chance, in Vienna.

"And what did he say?" Edith asked when he told her.

"We discussed Gall at some length." Fowler often spoke the names of more famous men, and Edith repeated the same names at night, before the mirror, in case the men arrived at the Institute as Fowler promised.

"What did he say about your head?"

"Well nothing, of course."

"He didn't read it? You didn't have him read it?"

"I'm far too sensitive," Fowler answered.

Fowler had examined Edith twice, declaring on the second examination that she did, perhaps, have an inclination toward his noble field. The rise in Edith's skull above her pronounced occipital bone indicated a well-developed faculty for learning and apprenticeship, and should she apply herself to her studies she would make a suitable companion to a renowned scientist. She had a great love of life, a passion for existence, which Fowler admitted to finding most attractive.

At night Edith practiced in the privacy of her home: on herself, her daughter, and heads conjured from memory. While Letty cooked supper and Grandpa searched vainly for his tobacco, Edith rediscovered herself by probing the bumps and indentations beneath her thick brown hair. She had a strong sense of color, she learned, a finding that prompted her to boldly match blues and scarlet with a long-treasured mustard scarf from Paris. And she had a great facility for judging time: its passing and relation to circumstance. With skill, she deduced the exact date of her husband's departure, a Thursday, just past Easter, early that year. She'd not seen Morris since the thirtieth of March.

AT DINNER GRANDPA sat at the dining table beside a stew pot of boiled cabbage and leeks. He wore his knit cap and regarded Edith in silence. He could no longer demand that she abandon her work, not now that she was grown and married, though in an indirect way his demands — don't work at the prison, don't involve yourself in politics or in teaching, my dear, you must marry and have children — had led to the discovery of her new talent. Grandpa had always known what was best for her.

Letty had laid out the good china. Behind her the fire provided light, but not heat enough to prevent the green-brown soup from cooling before the first drops reached the dinner bowls.

"Greens are good for the digestion," she said, dropping a second ladleful of vegetables into Grandpa's bowl. She'd dressed in one of her mother's old gowns, maroon with lace at the neck and cuffs, and she'd found her deceased grandmother's jewelry chest, from which she'd helped herself to a silver, rose-shaped brooch.

Grandpa gazed at the floor, where his most treasured volume, *An Experimental Inquiry into the Laws of the Vital Functions*, lay carelessly spread. The corner of the upturned page had torn, the paper stained with vegetable pulp. He stirred his stew, unable to bring even a spoonful to his lips.

Edith, who'd eaten across from Fowler at one of the Institute's most romantic lab tables, had no appetite either. Over a slab of sharp milk cheese and a jar of imported pickle, she and Fowler had discussed the human mind in great depth. She still felt submerged in the conversation.

Only Letty devoured the congealing soup, her gusto punctuated with unladylike grunts, which she stated "opened the esophagus and cleansed the internals."

"Boiled greens in such quantity will certainly interfere with the workings of the large intestine," Grandpa said, though neither of his companions acknowledged him.

It was he who first saw the letter, folded inside the *New York Observer*. The hand that addressed the envelope, precise yet utterly lacking in beauty, had spelled "Edith" in large letters, without adding "Tucker" beside it, the type of careless informality that only Morris would never think to question. The envelope, battered and torn at the side, had released its contents somewhere between Wisconsin and Orchard Street.

"From your dear husband," Grandpa said.

Edith, roused from her reverie, reached across the table to take the letter from Grandpa's indifferent fingers. She spread the empty envelope smooth on the table and gazed down as if divining the former contents from the address alone.

"He must be returning," Grandpa did not trouble to conceal the glee in his voice, "to collect you."

Letty set down her spoon. Stew stained the front of her dress, and her teeth were patterned with flecks of green. "I will not go to Wisconsin," she said.

"He should arrive any day now!" Grandpa announced,

setting his *Observer* over his soup. "Wisconsin is a fine place, Letty, a fine place for a girl like you."

Edith folded the envelope and held it close to her chest. Had the past months changed Morris? Would he be the same man he'd been before he set out?

EDITH MARRIED MORRIS Tucker under the lukewarm approval of her family and the utter disregard of his. The two exchanged vows at the courthouse two months after she noticed she'd failed to menstruate, and however brief the engagement, her friends concurred that Edith and Morris belonged together. Morris had such soulful brown eyes. And Edith smiled so sweetly at him. It was high time she married, and she seemed happier with Morris than she'd been with Edmund, though her former suitor was a wealthy banker who would have given her an easier life.

Edith first met her father-in-law two weeks after Letty was born. A frontiersman, Morris's pa left his wife six months before Morris came into the world. He returned to Cayuga County twenty-three years later, after Wild Man Briggs blinded him in a brawl. Though he'd lived in the same four-room house for years, he forgot the distance between the wall and table, and he often fell down the two steps leading to his front door.

"I lived off whiskey and raw bear meat for ten days." The blind man, thin and angular and bald as a worn-out carpet,

bored Edith with stories of dark-haired Indians, rough living, and rowdy camaraderie. "But when the rains stopped,
I speared up a coon with the arrow that got me. Didn't even
wipe the shaft off."

He showed scars on both forearms, from a knife or a long
Indian spear — he explained the injury both ways — and
bragged that he'd been so far north the water turned to ice
in mid-August.

"If I had my eyes," he said, "I'd be there still." Men
who lived on the edge, men who fought to the death, men
who rode hard through the night and slept but an hour
at dawn — these were the old man's heroes, a group he'd
stood proudly among till he lost his sight. Melancholy still
sounded in his voice.

Morris didn't note the many contradictions. He sat on
the floor, half a yard from his pa's bent knee, wide brown
eyes rimmed with his mother's long lashes, pale arms folded
around his soft torso. "The great wild's all been done," he
said later, as Edith tried vainly to lull Letty to sleep. The
Tucker house had more draughts than windows, and it
reeked of smoke and burnt porridge. "My pa did it," Morris
continued, "and now it's done."

For several weeks afterward, Morris sought adventure,
usually with a bottle of whiskey in hand and a rumpled
jacket slung over his shoulder. Insurance didn't suit him, he
said, though he did well enough in that profession to sup-

port his wife and daughter for the next twelve years, even to pay for music and voice lessons. Every few months he'd announce, "We're moving to the territories" or, "Us and Letty, we'll raise hogs and grow apples" or, "There's Indian wealth, the land. It's all been discovered, but we have it to settle. That's ours."

Edith was not about to leave New York for a remote town in the wilds where men still battled Indians. And since Morris would not plead or negotiate, the family stayed in their small house on Bleecker Street, where they would have remained had the elder Tucker not passed on.

The second time Edith saw Morris's pa, just under a year ago, the old man lay stretched out in a wooden box with his gun wrestled into the lifeless fingers of his left hand and a cowhide cord strung round his neck bearing a letter, penned in his uncertain, blind hand: "I sees you now."

Morris held the pall, front right, and he walked straight and proud until the boys at the rear pressed forward and he lost his footing and went down, right beside his pa's open grave. Edith screamed, thinking the old man and his box had killed her husband, but Morris stood up. He had a shiner the size of a clockface the next day, but that afternoon he gave his speech, speaking of his pa as if the old man had coddled him since the day he was born.

From then on Edith couldn't decide if the falling coffin had damaged Morris's brain or if, somehow, old Tucker's dead thoughts had slithered from the coffin and found a home in her husband's head. As soon as the family returned from the funeral, he stopped going to work, and he wouldn't respond when Edith scolded, entreated, promised butter cake and brandy, and at last, reached the end of her wits.

He spoke only to say that he was heading south to Texas to enlist in the militia. He wore his father's grin when he spoke of it, and he closed his eyes as if he were already blind, though more likely he imagined: the fights, the dust, the men who lived by cunning, not law, who drank beneath the morning sun or evening stars. He bought himself a rifle and a pair of black army boots. When Edith refused to sew him a jacket, he went out and bought one from the general store along with a hip flask and a canteen.

Edith burned the first jacket, stole the cap of his flask, removed his bootlaces. If she could delay him, she thought, for a week or two, his madness would pass. He would return to his insurance profession, for which he was well suited, as evidenced by the promotions he'd received over the years. He would support his family, who, though they did not yet feel the pinch of hard times, would rapidly descend into destitution without his salary. Besides, Morris had never shot a gun in his life, at least not to Edith's knowledge.

But the weeks passed and Morris only grew more determined. He'd lost his sense of hearing, didn't listen to a word

Edith said, until she brought up the territories. "What about Wisconsin?" she asked in a final attempt to dissuade him. "What about our plans to settle out west?"

"Letty and I will move in with Grandpa," she continued. "Just till you call for us. I know he won't mind." The fact that her father's house had thrice the rooms of the one she and Morris shared, as well as a generous yard, had not escaped her attention.

Morris agreed to head out west instead of south so quickly Edith might have thought he'd feigned his interest in the Texas militia to make her compromise. But, she knew, he'd just lost some part of his mind, that something in his head changed the day his father died. Did he need time? Could she turn him around? She asked her father, who assured her that the young man would benefit from a stint in a hyperbaric chamber — the pressure of submersion, especially in deep salt water, increased circulation, he said. Edith, who cared little for water and less for the ocean, decided to search for a cure herself. The first time she went to Fowler Corender's Institute, which promised to teach the only true science of the mind, she hoped she could learn enough to help Morris when he returned for her. She had not expected it to change her life.

For days after the empty envelope arrived, Letty prepared radishes, squash, and burnt apple for four.

She insisted that a place be set for her father, maintaining that a warm meal upon arrival would convince him to remain in New York.

The envelope itself took on meaning. The fact that it came after so many months of silence, without a surname, became evidence to Edith that Morris had taken up with another woman: a buxom girl with prairie dirt pressed deep in her skin.

Edith began to clean. She rearranged the boots and gloves and stockings in such a way that Grandpa could never find what he needed, and when he inquired, she admitted that she herself had forgotten. She swept the front porch six times a day, dusted the trim in the entryway, scrubbed the table and chairs, and at last, exhausted, failed to rise from her bed. "I'm happier without him," she said. Grandpa diagnosed her with a case of nerves, possibly even hysteria, for which he'd treated her on several previous occasions. He prescribed a dilute copper mineral solution, which Edith dutifully took four times a day, confident that her father's remedy would eventually cure her.

"If only Morris were here," she said. "If only an hour," an hour being, she determined, enough time to run her fingers over her husband's head to learn his true inclinations. She'd discovered much about herself that way, secret talents, unknown faults. Her husband's head, too, must have much to tell. And now that she could read man's true nature, she could not stand the thought of Morris running off without her hands first discovering his weakness, and dismissing him as a ne'er-do-well.

Grandpa assured her that Morris would arrive any day.

"You wouldn't want him to find you in bed," he said. "What kind of welcome is that?"

Edith was about to respond when a thundering knock drew her bolt upright. She ran her hands over her untended locks, which despite the tangles looked fetching around her pale cheeks. Letty, who had been searching for loose change in the pockets of Grandpa's desk, ran to the front door.

"Yes?" she said, breathless.

"I'm here for Edith Tucker."

Dismay arranged Letty's features in something close to a pout as she received the young Fowler and escorted him to her mother's bedside. Grandpa regarded the newcomer with irritation. The young man, ostentatiously dressed in a double-breasted jacket, silk cravat, and boots of fine leather, bowed deeply. He stepped forward to present his hand to Grandpa.

"Fowler Corender," he said.

Grandpa took the hand and, though he scarcely pressed it (a limp handshake being the vehicle through which he expressed distaste), Fowler pulled away.

"My hands are my work," he said. "Sensitive fingers for sensitive work."

"You've filled my daughter's head with your nonsense," Grandpa said, and though Edith tried to dismiss her father with a half-raised hand, he remained firmly beside her.

"Allow me to examine your head, my dear man, and you'll understand my profession." Fowler bent forward, his entire body assuming an emphatic nod. "The elderly and the feebleminded are always the last to adopt new ways."

Grandpa began to redden, his skin noticeably less wrinkled, as if displeasure had inflated his frame. Something changed in him then. Something that had been floating, like rotting wood, sank deep inside him.

"I've come to see Edith." Fowler brushed past the old man to his apprentice, who stared back with adoring eyes. "We've missed you at the Institute. What's ailing you, darling?" He spoke the endearment awkwardly, but with much affection.

"It's Morris," Edith said. "He wrote to say he'd be returning . . . or rather . . ."

"I'm very sorry," Fowler interrupted. "It must be terribly difficult, though death comes for us all in the end."

"Death!" cried Letty, who hovered in the doorway like a curious pup. Even Grandpa raised his brow in surprise.

"I'm not dying," Edith said.

"Of course you're not. There's nothing sentimental about you, Edith. Which is why I deduced that Morris had died. You have no need to explain further! Only death could send a strong woman like you to her bed." He patted Edith's hand and reached across the bed to wipe a strand of dark brown hair behind her ear. "But you are also the type to recover," his lips trembled, "quickly."

"Such nonsense!" Grandpa turned to Letty, who was crying softly. "Your father's alive and well and coming to fetch you. Shortly."

"I didn't realize—" Edith said. A new understanding crept into her voice. Of course Morris had died. Of course. A woman like her would not find herself bedridden for something so trivial as a mistress. Only death could explain her condition.

TRUE TO FOWLER'S assessment, Edith emerged from her bedroom the next day still pale but with a healthy appetite. Letty served unseasoned beets, claiming that both salt and pepper caused indigestion. The extra place setting was filled now by the dark-haired Fowler, who had called, dressed in his finest jacket and linen shirt, at the surprising request of Grandpa. "Tonight," the old man had written—a note he carried to the Institute himself—"I would like you to read my head."

Edith sat at the head of the table, one arm draped over her lap, the other extended and entwined in Fowler's, who had been so kind as to send flowers, in honor of life and love and the future of science.

"I'm delighted that you've agreed to the examination," Fowler said to Grandpa. "I've brought several charts, so as to demonstrate more clearly."

"Fowler Corender," Grandpa said, spooning his beets with unprecedented relish. He, too, had dressed for the evening, in a loose tailcoat with a deep red cravat, which had been the rage in London a decade earlier. He even smoothed the few gray hairs poking out from beneath his cap. "I've been looking forward to your visit all afternoon."

"Won't you read me?" Letty asked Fowler.

"Another time," Edith said. "We don't want to — "

"Perhaps tomorrow night," Fowler said. "Or the night after. There is nothing but time, my dear child."

Letty smiled and noted aloud that Fowler only poked at his beets.

"My senses are heightened by an empty stomach," he declared, pushing back from the table in an attempt, perhaps, to end the dinner and begin the night's true entertainment. "I become even more observant, more attuned to the sutures and bumps of the skull."

Grandpa nodded, reaching forward for a second helping. His spirits remained high when the party adjourned to the front parlor, where he sat in his favorite chair, empty at last of Edith's garments. The chandelier, lit for the first time in months, cast a warm light over the room. Even the rugs, swept clean, had a soft, welcoming hue.

"You must remove the cap," Fowler said, a request which Grandpa obliged, his head suddenly small and vulnerable.

From his pocket Fowler pulled a bottle of castor oil, which he rubbed liberally over his fingers. With the confidence of a man twice his age, he pressed his left and right thumb to Grandpa's cheekbones, running his fingers along the top of his head and over the external opening of each ear.

Letty played a few discordant notes on the harpsichord, which she maintained added drama.

"You have a rather large irritability organ," Fowler said, eyes closed in concentration. "And quite a developed sense of self-importance."

Though both Edith and Letty stared at Grandpa, awaiting an outburst from the old man, he remained calm. With his wide grin and gleaming eyes, he looked almost delighted.

"The last man I read with such a large posterior lobe was the finest butcher in New York," Fowler continued. He moved his hands forward and down, "And here, where we usually find intelligence—" Fowler paused, allowing a frown to possess his usually placid features, "There is a great imbalance. It seems the right hemisphere is much larger than the left. Which might point to a softening, or a lack of acuity, even among those faculties most expressed. Edith, darling, you must feel for yourself."

Edith accepted Fowler's outstretched hand, and stepped around to examine Grandpa. Fowler's invitation — the first ever — to share in a study brought a smile to her lips.

"You've deduced all of that from the lines of my head?" Grandpa asked.

"I know more about you than I would had I known you for years." Fowler ran a hand over the back of Edith's neck as he continued. "What we can learn of the mind, that mystery, heretofore shrouded, obscure."

"Isn't it wonderful?" Edith said, ostensibly to Grandpa, though her eyes were locked with Fowler's.

"You even determined that Morris is dead?"

"Other scientists might not be so bold as to deduce it," Fowler said, his voice swelling with confidence, "but that's where they're lacking."

"And you'd stake your reputation on it?"

"My reputation is far too large to wager."

"My daughter, then," Grandpa said. "If you're mistaken, you'll leave my daughter forever. And my daughter," he turned to Edith, "will leave my house, along with her boxes and bags and Letty."

"One should never bet against Doctor Corender," Edith said.

"You agree then?"

Edith had scarcely finished nodding, when Grandpa produced a letter from the pocket of his dinner jacket.

Though it was addressed to Edith, he'd taken the liberty of opening it. "From Morris," he said with a grandiose flourish, presenting the letter not to Edith but to Fowler. "Who is very much alive and well and anxious to reunite with his lovely wife and daughter. To take them *away*. It arrived today, by post."

"And what of it?" Fowler dismissed the letter without a glance at its contents. "Edith's not well suited for that ruffian Morris. If his death was not real, it was certainly symbolic. Their marriage is unbearable. Unthinkable. Anyone would agree that the two must divorce."

Grandpa's grin faded, and he brushed Edith's fingers from his head.

"Besides, Edith has agreed to work with me," Fowler continued.

"It's true. Fowler and I were just discussing the Institute. It's growing rapidly, and we have so much room here."

"Certainly not," Grandpa said.

"But of course you'll allow it." Edith stepped forward, beside Fowler, who was stretching the rim of the old man's cap. She brushed her hair back, fingers gliding over the subtle contours of her skull. She had diagnosed her father. When she bent and touched the old man's shoulder, she, too, spoke with the authority of science. "I read it in your head."

 The Baquet

There's a fool out on Neglect Pier," Parkhurst said, pointing over crowds of dockworkers to the old wharf across from Salton's anchor and tackle shop.

"Birds won't even land there." Quimbly swallowed the last of the apple he'd stolen on Canal Street, throwing the core into the Hudson, whose foamy scum consumed it. Whoever the Fool was, he'd stepped over the log barrier. Unperturbed by the stench of rotting wood and fish, he'd unfolded a long table covered in angular gold symbols.

"Looks like he's gonna preach something." Parkhurst stepped closer, his freckled face pink from too much sun. A small crowd had gathered around Neglect Pier: burly men in brown trousers and open cotton shirts, and dozens of redheaded foreigners, traveling cases in hand, too new to figure north from south. Quimbly had so stood months earlier, at last striking out along the river, past cast-iron fences, docks, junk shops, warehouses, and sail lofts, till he found the shantytown near Thirty-seventh Street. He'd met Parkhurst and the others — Cobb, Phineas, and John Bovee — crouched around a fire with a live chicken and not the first clue how to pluck it. Under the moonlight and the glaring red of the foundries, Quimbly cracked the bird's neck, and he'd fallen in with the boys ever since.

"C'mon," Parkhurst said. Crowds meant easy money, and Parkhurst had a knack for picking pockets. He'd killed a man, too, kept the bloody knife, wrapped in a lady's silk scarf, back at the hideout as proof. Quimbly was the better listener. He would discover which ships were coming in, what cargo each carried, and when they would dock. He liked to think of himself as an ear to Parkhurst's criminal mastermind. Being ears was much easier than baling cotton, carting chickens, or digging canals, all of which he had tried over the two years since he'd run away from home.

The Fool threw a gold velvet cloth over the tabletop and turned to reveal that there were not one but two people out on the pier: the Fool and a woman who wore pearls in her ears and a fur-trimmed red satin gown.

"If they fall through, we'll nick that chest." Parkhurst nodded toward the blue travel trunk from which the Fool plucked a wondrous jacket, silver and gold and pink and yellow in shimmering vertical stripes. He tossed it around his shoulders, made a cone with his hands, and called out.

"Greetings." His voice had a musical quality, and even this simple word had a melody. The catfish cart wheeled closer, old Sal stepped away from his bait store, and the bird lady, who spent each afternoon feeding the pigeons, stopped throwing crumbs. Parkhurst winked and slipped into the crowd.

"You gentlemen look like a healthy lot, but that doesn't mean you don't know someone sickly. Don't know a poor hopeless soul. Perhaps you've been told that there's no cure for Grandmother's madness? For your uncle's bad back? For your wife's, or lady friend's, private disease?"

On most days, the furious pace of waterfront traffic — coaches and hacks laden with cotton and reckless omnibuses tearing through narrow streets with thundering horse hooves and angry cries — would have drowned the Fool's words, left him standing unheeded in the midday sun. No traveling salesman could compete with the local hawkers, men who spoke as loud as gunshots and drove hard bargains for boot blacking or flavored ice. But the Fool had managed, and Quimbly pushed toward the log barrier. Of his shantytown companions, he was the best traveled, and he prided himself that he alone had seen three states, dairy farms and countryside, mountains and beaches, a woman with two heads, a man who dressed up like a lady, and two sets of identical twins. But the Fool was something entirely new. He and his lady companion, whose dark eyelashes and dangling pearls appeared even more beautiful as Quimbly neared, had a special charisma.

"I'm Doctor Steenwycks, and this is my assistant, Ada." The Fool no longer cupped his hands, and his voice traveled unaided across the waterfront, luring sailors from as far as three piers away. "What we're here to tell you is that your doctor hasn't the vaguest understanding of his art. What we're here to tell you is what men like Charles Dickens already know, what great men like Uldericus Balk and Maximilian Hell preached for years: animal magnetism."

Quimbly felt a girl's breath on his cheek — Bettine, standing so close he could smell her — fried egg, sweat, boiled spinach. Why did she follow him? Out of all the boys? She and her mother, a stern German woman who seemed too old to have a daughter, had moved to a tagrag hut between Eleventh Avenue and the rocky, corncob-strewn shore of the Hudson a few days ago. Neither spoke English. Now the girl spent her days following Quimbly. She smiled, teeth small and even. Her eyes were hazel, he realized, big as quarters. He'd never seen her up close before. She was pretty. Oddly pretty and just his age, he guessed, thirteen.

"Animal magnetism," the Fool repeated. He took a long sip from a glass Ada offered. "There must be one among you with an illness of some sort. Headache? A disorder of the eyes?"

From behind, Quimbly heard, "I've got a headache," and he turned to the unshaven sailor in short-torn trousers. He would fall through the pier, he must know. His bare calves had more muscle than most men's shoulders. But the sailor stepped over the rail without hesitation.

"A headache, you say?" The Fool directed the man to lie down on the velvet-clad table. The wharf creaked and listed to the left, but the Fool proceeded, running his hands over the sailor's forehead.

"What most doctors don't know is that the universe is fluid. That air, and water, sand, even solid wrought iron, have fluidity. Different degrees. And man can act on these fluids, force his will upon them. You see, my friends, this matter I speak of is not complex. In fact, if you listen, if you understand, you'll find your life far simpler. Far more manageable. How do you feel, my friend?" The Fool spoke to his patient, but the audience responded, overlapping cries of "grand" and "swell."

The sailor sat up, his eyes partially closed, lids floating over an unfocused stare. He held his right hand open, palm raised to the Fool and said, "I feel well."

Ada clapped, her fingers flashing with diamond rings, and the audience roared with delight. Quimbly's palms burned from applauding, which he could no longer remember beginning. He turned to find Bettine, to share the thrill with a smile, but she no longer stood beside him.

"He feels well!" the Fool sang, the words tumbling like a

blessing from his lips. The day seemed brighter and warmer. Ada held forth a blue silk bag into which the sailor emptied the contents of his wallet. Her smile broadened. She held the crowd between her lovely red lips.

"Help us spread the cure, the truth," she cried. "Help us build the baquet."

The Fool spun beside her, his dazzling stripes blurring to form a blanket of color. "Help us build the baquet!" he echoed. "We need your help to build the baquet. Tomorrow. Tompkins Square. Tell your friends!"

The silk bag passed before Quimbly, but he had nothing to slip into it, and he looked away as Ada swept by. He had never seen a baquet, didn't even know what one looked like, but the urgency of the Fool's request filled him, and he, like the rest of the onlookers, recognized the importance of the thing. The Fool and the sailor were shaking hands now. The pier shook.

"Quimbly, chum!"

Quimbly turned, recognizing Parkhurst as if for the first time in many months. His friend wore a new beige scarf and carried a lady's handbag.

"If you made off with half what I did . . ." Parkhurst pulled two leather wallets from an inside pocket of his jacket along with a gold chain and an engraved locket. "And better still," he bent close to whisper, "I heard the *Sea Witch* is docking two days hence. Loaded with gold from California!"

THAT NIGHT QUIMBLY was the last to arrive at the hideout, a rocky stretch of shore protected by a dozen yards of abandoned dock. Parkhurst had already begun outlining plans, and Cobb, Phineas, and John Bovee sat round him, eager to learn the nature of the coming crime. The darkness hid their faces and the color of their clothes, but Quimbly could tell them apart: John, the fat one whose back sloped like the shell of an egg; Cobb, who claimed to be eleven, though he stood no taller than a six-year-old, and Phineas, Cobb's older brother, who at fifteen was the oldest of the lot. The River Gang, they called themselves, and beside them, their upturned rowboat looked much like the surrounding boulders.

"Password?" Parkhurst said, and Quimbly knew that his friend's pale blue eyes had found his shadowy form. The Hudson met the dock post with burps and splatters of cold water that on windy nights rose high enough to catch even Parkhurst, who always sat on the largest rock.

"California."

"You're late."

"Don't got a watch." Quimbly slipped under the dock and sat beside John Bovee. He didn't want to admit that he'd been eating with Bettine and her mother. The girl had found him skipping rocks, taken his hand, and brought him fireside, where Frau Klein fried eggs and served him hot cabbage and potatoes from a chipped ceramic pot. Bettine made him lie down, and she ran her hands over him just like the Fool had the sailor a few hours before. He'd watched her fingers, the smallest encircled by a scrap of red cloth, ends tied to resemble a rose.

"No watch?" Parkhurst laughed and the other boys followed, tearing the night with their mirth. "Here, take one of mine. You can pay me later." He tossed a cold metal oval at Quimbly, who caught it and stuck it into his one good pocket.

"We've planned it all out," Parkhurst continued. "Wednesday, Cobb and Phineas and me and you will take the boat out, before daybreak, when it's darkest. We'll board the *Sea Witch* stern side, and slip into the hold, all of us except Cobb, who'll stay with the rowboat. He's too small to carry much anyway. And John Bovee will be on shore watch."

"I'm always on watch," John Bovee said.

"We need to have room for the gold." Parkhurst bent forward and the others pulled closer to listen, "I hear there's nuggets as big as my head."

"What if they catch you?" Cobb pulled his torn jacket tighter, the shirtsleeves dangling over his fingertips.

"Won't happen." Parkhurst reached behind him to pull out his murder knife, which he tapped, blunt side against his knee. "First off, no one's expecting us to row out. Second, ain't no one awake at that hour, and third, if there is, I'll take care of him."

"Me too," Phineas said, though his words rang hollow.

Quimbly rubbed his new pocket watch. The thought of the icy Hudson terrified him, though he would never admit it, nor the fact that he couldn't swim. He was still new to the River Gang, still proving himself. He knew the boys liked him for the very reason they were wary of him: he was traveled, adventurous. To contradict this image would upset them. His words would hold less authority, and he knew what happened when one lost authority. Knew from the example of his father, a preacher now behind bars for thieving, though no one would have raised even an eyebrow had he not admitted, one drunken afternoon before his congregation, to meeting Satan. His wife, Quimbly's ma, had slept with too many dairy farmers to have much authority either. Quimbly knew better. "What about the docks?" he said.

"John'll whistle three times if he sees anything. We'll row out whichever way's safe." Parkhurst nodded, the motion of his head and shoulder a dark blur. "Tomorrow night, we practice."

"It's a good plan," Phineas confirmed, brushing the dirt from his trousers and rising. "We'll be rich."

"Wait!" Parkhurst held forth his knife, one hand on the handle, the other cradling the blade, and Phineas bent to kiss it. Cobb and John Bovee followed, then Quimbly, who, like the others, did it because it brought good luck. The moon, just a ribbon, hung low enough that it shone blue in the metal.

"May the *Sea Witch* bring great riches." Parkhurst looked down, as if praying, and Quimbly could make out the lines of his friend's narrow lips, which opened and closed around each word with practiced precision. Soon Parkhurst would scratch a new line beside the dozen or so that marked each meeting.

"May —" Parkhurst turned suddenly, raising his knife. "Who's there!"

Feet crunched beach gravel. All five boys turned, discovered the small, dark figure a few yards away. Within seconds Phineas held the intruder pinned between his arm and chest. "Who are you? What are you doing here?" he demanded.

"You'll wake all of New York!" Parkhurst stepped forward to take the intruder from Phineas's rough embrace. The outline of a skirt swirled, and Parkhurst leaned forward to regard the sniffling creature. "It's that German girl," he said. "Must have followed you, Quimbly."

"How do you know?" Quimbly stared at Bettine, but he couldn't tell if her eyes met his. She'd get him in a lot of trouble if she hadn't already.

"We all came from downtown."

"Wasn't me." Quimbly said, but Bettine had recognized him. She stepped tearfully beside him, her hand seeking his.

"How much she hear?" Cobb asked.

"Don't matter now," John Bovee tossed a rock into the river, allowing the thunk to introduce his conclusion. "Now we've got to kill her."

"She didn't understand. Can't speak a word of English." Quimbly knocked Bettine's hand away so that she'd know not to follow him again. He raised an arm against John's intentions. Quimbly didn't much care for violence, especially to girls. And contradicting John Bovee was easy, as no one ever listened to him.

Parkhurst swung his knife. He laughed and stepped close to Bettine. Words rushed from her lips, harsh, quick, German words, the sounds tumbling over each other like children over fallen change.

"You won't say nothing to no one, you hear?" Parkhurst said and then tucked the knife into his back pocket, perhaps too quickly, because he added: "I don't want to hurt you, but I will next time." He turned to the others. "Come on."

"What about — " John Bovee began.

"Quimbly's sweet on her."

"Am not," Quimbly called as the others headed back along the waterfront. Bettine took his hand again, and he was glad for the darkness concealing his blush.

THE MEMORY OF the Fool's voice drew Quimbly to Thompkins Square the next morning, after a hasty breakfast of stale rolls and fried fish swiped from a stand. The crowd surpassed the one assembled the day before, though the dockworkers now wore clean, buttoned shirts and held children or called after ones running screaming through trampled flower beds. Even the fashionable ladies, arriving from the surrounding brownstones in white gloves and tulle-covered hats, trod upon the soil to steal a better view. The Fool knew people in high places, Quimbly decided.

The Fool wore wide gold-colored suspenders and a top hat that towered high. He seemed to dance as he pulled a dark metal rod from his traveling trunk and circled the old elm near the park's center. Ada held one of the tree's snaking roots, thick as her arm and the color of frosty soil. Her hair, fastened back in a braid and tied with blue ribbons, was shiny. She appeared tired to Quimbly, who noted her pallor and the red lips that not once turned up to smile. She bent gracefully, nodding politely when the Fool asked if she "felt it," but her heart seemed elsewhere. The Fool, on the other hand, tied rope with zeal, dozens of eight-yard lengths that he spread along the ground to radiate from the tree trunk like the spokes of a wheel.

Quimbly leaned forward to observe the frayed end of the strand nearest him. He reached out to touch it, but a cold hand pulled him away.

"Let the sick forward." An old woman glared at him

from a Merlin chair with large, mud-covered wheels and a padded back and footrest. Dressed head to toe in gray delaine, she looked like an insect. "Move aside, boy."

And though Quimbly had no desire to comply, her two sons, dockworkers both of them and strong enough to heft crates of coffee and flour single-handedly, pulled him away.

"I've waited nearly two hours," Quimbly began, but the Fool announced himself, and the crowd applauded and Quimbly fell back yet again.

"This is Ada, my lovely assistant." The Fool's voice rose, sweet syrup to the hungry. "She will join today with the sick and find cure! For though heavenly in aspect, she is diseased. Insomnia! Nights without the pleasure of dream! Waking hours of cold darkness, solitude. Who will join with her today? Who, too, will find peace of body and mind?"

Ada tied a cord around her waist. She raised one arm and regarded the crowd with eyes made no less beautiful by the dark circles beneath them.

"We men are like magnets," the Fool continued. "We act on other bodies, we propel matter through space. We are fluid, natural, one with all celestial — Wait!" He held his hand to the crowd. "Do not mock my words. Do not disregard their truth. Open yourselves to the force, the magnetic energy emanating from this elm. Allow it to join with you, to flow through you, to heal your wounds and troubles. Listen to me. Listen to my words."

The spidery gray lady grasped the rope, as did nearly a dozen others, older people mostly, aside from Ada and a young girl with a harelip. Quimbly longed to take hold of a rope as well. The Fool's words had uncovered a roughness inside him, a feeling that throbbed like an empty stomach. He felt foolish, uncertain. If he'd been a child, he'd have run to his mother.

"I've magnetized this tree with my most powerful magnet. The force will flow through you, align your humors. Remember, the magnetized compass needle points north, while its poleless counterpart spins aimlessly. Come, join me!" The Fool led the roped patients — he, pushing the old lady's wheeled chair, the others, stepping slowly, mostly with eyes closed, expectant. Forward and back. Quimbly could not look away.

"I'm healed!" a gaunt man cried, flexing his fingers in front of his eyes. One after another, the patients released their ropes, meeting Ada, who had stepped away from the tree to collect payments in her blue silk bag. The old woman attempted to rise from her wheeled chair, and the Fool put his arms around her, guiding her upward, forward.

"Once the internal harmony has faltered," he said — he'd been speaking for some minutes now, Quimbly realized, only he couldn't remember the words — "we must re-establish the natural state. The healthy state. That is to say, disease is nothing but interference. Matter interfering with fluid."

"I have not felt so good in years," the old lady said, though her legs gave way and she fell back into her cushioned seat. "Years!

"If only I had the baquet!" the Fool answered, speaking over her head to the crowd. "There's no substance more fluid, more capable of conducting, than water. But we need a baquet."

"Help us build a baquet!" Ada echoed. And as she had the day before, she gathered contributions, this time hundreds of folded bills and silver coins.

Quimbly found a stretch of shaded ground and sat, watching strangers engage the Fool in conversation: Will it work for rheumatism? For chronic pain? For toothache? Blindness? Upset stomach? Even Quimbly could answer the questions, a boy who could neither read nor write, who stole his breakfast and slept under the stars with a rusted saucer that served as a pillow.

At last only the Fool and Ada remained, and Quimbly approached them, his hair combed as best he could with fingers, his face wiped clean with palms and spit. "I'd like to apprentice," he said before he realized that he'd waited till all the others left in order to say just this. He could taste the words, like suckers dissolving on his tongue. An unexpected sweetness.

The Fool regarded Quimbly with a half smile. Up close

his skin looked windburned. "You could use a good bath, a bit of soap," he said.

Quimbly stared back at him, hands in pockets. Now that he'd spoken his unformed desire, he could think of nothing else.

"You have great animal magnetism. I sense this about you. You draw people, don't you?" The Fool did not wait for an answer. "You were drawn to me. But you must realize that I practice with powerful forces. Cosmic forces. Not the sort one takes or gives lightly."

Ada ran her hand over the Fool's shoulder. "I could use a rest, love," she said.

"A rest from the bottle." The Fool tousled the boy's hair. "You must promise, on the blood of your ancestors, and your own if you have no one else, to do good. Solely good. Not one false step. Not one careless word! When you practice my art, you control your listener. Do you hear me? Do you really hear me? Do you understand?"

Warmth coursed through Quimbly despite the chill of spring dusk. His eyes felt heavy, his lips tried to open but could not.

"You must not use the power for selfish gain. You must not abuse it. Not once. Do you hear?"

Quimbly tried to nod, felt the muscles but not the motion. Had he answered?

"Very good," the Fool said. "Tomorrow, then. Noon at

62 Orchard Street. My dear sister has invited us to perform a cure. Bathe first." The Fool removed his top hat, revealing damp curls that spiraled around his forehead. "Buy yourself something to eat," he added kindly, handing Quimbly a wad of folded bills. "And a smart outfit."

THAT NIGHT, AT MIDNIGHT, under a cloud-covered sliver of moon, was the practice run. Parkhurst and Phineas, the largest of the five boys, carried the rowboat to the river's edge, and Cobb, who noticed the missing oar, raced off to steal one from a nearby pier.

The water looked blacker than usual to Quimbly, and especially cold, as he remembered he'd have to bathe in it the next morning. His parcel, containing new trousers, shirt, and a black stovepipe hat, sat concealed among the rocks. He hadn't returned to the shantytown for fear of finding Bettine, whom he'd managed to avoid all day. He tied his face mask, torn from an old jacket lining Parkhurst brought, and tried to look confident as he stepped into the rowboat.

John Bovee refused to steady the boat, a passive protest against his status as watchman, but Quimbly made his way to the front beside Parkhurst. Behind him Phineas and Cobb argued, the older brother claiming that the younger's strokes scarcely touched the water, forcing the boat to turn constantly starboard. The river moved differently in the darkness, as stealthy as a burglar, and strong. But the four soon found a rhythm, learned the current.

"We'll have to be faster tomorrow," Parkhurst said, his oar balanced on his knees.

Tomorrow Quimbly would see 62 Orchard Street. The address alone evoked a happiness as bright as a fresh, plucked fruit. He'd learn how to make magic with his voice, how to hold people trancelike, how to cure and control them.

"Quimbly!" Parkhurst said. "Mind the dock." And Quimbly ducked just in time to avoid colliding with the wooden rail at the side of a low pier.

"I didn't see," Quimbly said.

"Be alert. We can't afford mistakes."

The admonition delighted Cobb and Phineas, who received Parkhurst's displeasure so often they rejoiced when it fell on other shoulders. Quimbly shifted his weight; the boat dipped. Mistakes happened only when he lied. If truth was on his side, as his father used to say when he was sober, so was everything else, and there was no way he could go wrong. He searched for the words to explain this, to assure Parkhurst that everything would work out. "I don't make mistakes," was all he could come up with.

From the shore came three low whistles: John Bovee reporting a constable or night watchman. "Come on," Parkhurst said.

"It's not really an alarm is it?" Cobb said. "I mean —"

"Pull," Parkhurst commanded. "Pull hard."

The boys pushed off from the dock and rowed toward the hideout to the rhythm of Parkhurst's hissed disappointments: Your heart must be in it. I can't be minding you. You can't be whining, or dreaming, or picking your nose. There's thousands of dollars of gold to be had. Are you in? All in?

Quimbly felt his friend's demanding stare. Cold water leaked into the bottom of the boat, a half inch, but enough to wet his feet and send a chill through his body.

"You haven't been the same since you lost your heart to that girl," Parkhurst continued.

"I did not." Quimbly's voice wavered. Bettine meant nothing to him, despite her soulful eyes and hair that always looked neat though she slept on a filthy pink blanket and didn't own a mirror. "She follows me around."

"Your head's so full you practically lost it on that dock back there." The boat struck the riverbank, and Parkhurst jumped out to pull it ashore. "We might have to put you on dock watch."

Cobb and Phineas laughed.

"I'm in," Quimbly said, words he hoped sounded convincing. Soon he would stand on land again, and he'd feel more in control. "All in."

◆ ◆ ◆

THE HOUSE AT 62 Orchard Street, even grander inside than out, had carpeted floors and chandeliers that hung like sparkling gems from the ceiling. Embroidered curtains framed tall windows, and a dark-skinned girl stood beside the door to sweep the step so that it was fresh for each arriving guest. The house was an institute, a special hospital for the head. Quimbly couldn't read the sign, but he overheard two gentlemen speak of it, and the fact that Caroline Stone brought all her suitors for a reading before she would receive them in her home.

The front parlor contained nearly twenty guests, Quimbly estimated, trying not to stare at any of the finely dressed men and women. A dark-haired woman — the Fool's sister, most likely — was greeting each arrival and handing out pamphlets. She wore four gold necklaces and as many gold rings on each hand, and she didn't even look when a heavy-set woman hailed her urgently from across the room; she shook her head and said, "Not now, Letty," nothing more, even when Letty dropped the tray of dried plums she'd been holding and stomped away, leaving the fruits to roll over the floor.

The Fool, fingers dampened with spit, played an old-fashioned glass harmonica, left foot pumping the worn wooden pedal, fingers rubbing the instrument glass with great fondness. The soft notes hung behind genteel conversations about weather and riding, miracle cures, and the latest fashion.

"Bit late," the Fool said.

"You said noon." Quimbly felt small, despite his top hat and clean red shirt fastened with real cufflinks snatched secretly from Parkhurst's stash. He glanced around the room again, searching for Ada, but finding no one quite so glamorous even among the ladies in lovely silk gowns, with lockets — all of them — around pale necks.

The Fool nodded toward the guests as if to apologize for his assistant's tardiness. "Ada's ill, or rather, she's refused cure this morning. A half hour with the baquet is all she needs. But she heard no reason."

"The baquet?"

The Fool abruptly stopped playing and smiled, and Quimbly stepped back to examine the man completely. He looked more distinguished than ever in a tailcoat and pressed trousers. His fingers, long and pale and relaxed despite the quick notes they created, seemed to belong to the instrument.

He kicked a canvas bag the size of a small dog toward Quimbly. "Iron filings," he said. "Go on. Make yourself useful."

Quimbly picked up the heavy canvas sack and followed the Fool to the center of the room where sat a large oak vat nearly six feet across and perhaps a quarter as tall. Where had the Fool found the device? The wood of the baquet had aged and darkened on the inside, which was filled with water. Submerged bottles, arranged in concentric circles, pointed either toward the center or the rim of the vat, where two dozen iron rods projected, each bent at the end to form a handle.

"Fold that," the Fool said, tossing the gold velvet cloth that had covered the vat. "No, leave it for now. We have to stir in the filings. Inside this vat, we have magnetized water. The very finest magnetized water, some from as far away as southern France."

At first Quimbly thought the Fool was explaining only to him, but as the Fool introduced himself and his assistant, "the boy," Quimbly realized that the show had begun, and he hastened to mix the filings into the tub.

"Step round. Gather round!"

Quimbly raised one arm, just as Ada had, and grabbed hold of an iron rod. The metal was far warmer than his skin, almost so hot that he released it.

"Sore from riding? Exhausted from last night's capers? Pain, sickness. Enough! Behold the baquet." The Fool's words echoed off the walls. Quimbly was meant to hear that voice, meant to learn the healing art, which he knew would, once he'd mastered it, forever assure him respect.

Quimbly raised his arm again and bowed slightly as the audience turned to him. He could see whose eyes had already partially closed and who still gazed at the baquet skeptically. Soon they too would understand. He smiled, certain that the chandelier light glittered in his cufflinks.

"Come, join my assistant at its side. Feel the force of magnetic fluid. Shed your complaints, your burdensome worries. Embrace somnambulism, let me be your guide."

Each grasping hand added depth, a new vibration to the heat of the baquet. The woman in the china-patterned dress across from Quimbly felt as close as the bareheaded gentleman behind him. The rod burned in his fingers, but he could not release it. His hand had a will of its own, a creature apart from his body, a thing that responded only to the Fool's dulcet voice.

"Create a circuit! Join hands! Feel the energy flow through you."

Quimbly no longer felt his body. The woman in front of him began convulsing, her chest heaving violently. Laughter and sobs nearly drowned the Fool's words: Relax, he said, give way to the forces. Small waves formed on the surface of the water. The submerged bottles began to shake, to strike each other with dull thuds. Quimbly was laughing. Joy coursed through his body, threw his small frame forward, into the full peach skirt of his neighbor.

The room had grown lighter, the water steamed. "The baquet!" Quimbly cried, though he did not recognize his voice. "The baquet."

And then it was over. He fell to the floor alongside the fine gentlemen and ladies. He felt breathless, as if he'd run for miles. He lacked the energy to rise when the Fool offered his hand.

"Come along now," the Fool said, calm but firm. "This house is not so wonderful as it might seem."

"What happened?" Quimbly said. "I've forgotten —"

"Men often forget." The Fool handed Quimbly a mop and bucket.

Men, Quimbly thought. He'd never been called by that word before. Through the window, he was surprised to see that night had fallen.

QUIMBLY SCARCELY HAD time to return to the shantytown to exchange his fine clothes for a dark shirt and trousers before he raced to the dock for the predawn gold run. His legs felt numb and his thoughts unclear, but his pocket watch still held the afternoon's magnetic charge, and he wrapped his palm around the warm metal. He remembered little; only the moment he collected change and the Fool tore the bag from his hands with a firm whisper, "Do not ask for money here!"

The Fool had lectured him about audiences and expectations, his voice no different from Parkhurst's when he became mad. But then he spoke of constellations and planets and the relations of all things to each other, this time to Quimbly alone, and the boy was quick to promise the Fool that he'd help set up the baquet at eight the next morning.

"Where've you been?" Parkhurst demanded. He and the others had already tied their masks and the boat was upright and drawn to the river edge.

"Work," Quimbly said.

"Work? Not lollygagging with that girl?" Parkhurst laughed and hit Quimbly's shoulder with what might have been a friendly tap except for the force behind it. "After tonight, we'll be rich! Rich beyond belief. And you go to work. Did you hear that? Quimbly, at work."

"I'm here now," Quimbly said. He felt older than the other boys, or at least more knowledgeable.

"Are you coming?" Parkhurst unwrapped his knife with a flourish of dirty cloth. "You said you were in."

Quimbly slipped into his seat and took the waiting oar. He did not want to go out on the river again; Parkhurst's scheme, the whole notion of the River Gang, no longer seemed enticing. But if he backed out now, he'd be yellow forever.

Parkhurst held his knife between his knees, blade pointed skyward as the rowboat made its way to the looming hull of the *Sea Witch*. She had lost half a mast on her journey and floated like a large broken bird alongside the low pier that had nearly taken Quimbly's head the night before. The rig was dark, lighted by neither oil nor gas lamp. A loose rope flapped against the deck, and water hit the bowed side, plangent beats that soon had all four boys breathing in rhythm.

Cobb tied the rowboat to the rung of the rope ladder running up the ship's stern. Parkhurst started up first, and silent and smooth as shadows, Phineas and Quimbly followed. Quimbly counted the rungs, repeating the numbers under his breath to keep focused. The ship rocked gently.

"Easy," Parkhurst whispered. The *Sea Witch* seemed abandoned, without even a guard. "Easy as picking pockets."

"Sh!" Phineas, alert and tense despite the vessel's emptiness, inched toward the cabin. Only the shore light reached them, a faraway glow.

"We're just yards away from —"

"Quiet!" Phineas nearly yelled this time, and the three froze, listening for John Bovee's warning whistle. A gull took flight from the foremast. Far below, Quimbly thought he heard Cobb sniffle. Seconds passed, then Parkhurst nodded and the three moved forward.

"Here it is," Parkhurst said. The hold was unlocked, open even, the wood cold and salty. The boys stepped, hands forward and searching, into its musty depths.

"I'm going to buy my own boat and sail round the world." Parkhurst moved deeper into the darkness, his voice muffled.

"I'm building a castle," Phineas declared. "And only the River Gang is invited."

"If I had a lump of gold as large as my head," Quimbly began, though he realized that he hadn't once thought about what he'd do with the treasure. He imagined burying the nugget in the ground, secreted away from everyone except, perhaps, Bettine, who couldn't tell anyone. He considered showing the Fool, asking if he could magnetize it — all thoughts he would never share with the others.

"I found it!" Phineas interrupted. "Tons of it!"

Long and hard and thick as his thigh, the lumps of metal felt warm to Quimbly who ran his hands over them. Parkhurst reached down to lift a small chunk, but stumbled beneath the weight.

"Give me a hand," he said.

But Quimbly, who felt the pull of the metal, silenced him. "It's pig iron," he said. "It's all pig iron."

PARKHURST WOULD NOT leave empty-handed, though the rowboat rode so low in the water that the Hudson poured over the sides. The misshapen iron rested between the benches, rolling back and forth as the boat lurched forward. The breeze had picked up, and the sky glowed with the soft light of the sun still tucked beneath the horizon.

"Riches," Phineas muttered. "That's the last time I listen to you."

Beside him Parkhurst pulled so fiercely and single-mindedly that it was not till many minutes had passed that he realized he'd left his knife on the ship. By then the rowboat was too full of water to turn back.

"I can't swim," Cobb whimpered. "Can't swim a stroke."

"Me neither," Quimbly said, admitting the weakness absently. The boat, he realized, was nothing less than a baquet. A floating vat with water, iron, and wooden sides. He felt warm where the water engulfed his shoes and ankles and splashed his fingertips. The heat spread through his chest and throat. He couldn't swim, his boat was sinking, and he'd returned empty-handed, but he felt grand. "Don't worry." The shore stretched before them, twenty long yards away. They'd reach it. Even Cobb must know. "We're aligned, don't you see?"

A figure, crouched by the rocks, stood to greet them, and Parkhurst spoke for the first time since leaving the *Sea Witch*. "Good God, Quimbly." The harsh syllables nearly broke the musical spell. "It's that girl."

Quimbly searched the shore, found the silhouetted form. Even in shadow Bettine looked pretty, and as they rowed closer he could make out her smile, her hopeful expression. She carried an oar, as if awaiting an invitation.

"*Das Boot*," she said, pointing toward the *Sea Witch*.

"I'd kill her, but I don't have my knife." Parkhurst slapped the water with his oar and jumped out. Quimbly followed, the two tugging the boat to the rocks.

"She'll forget," Quimbly said. "I know how to make her."

"You're a fool," Parkhurst said, "a damned, bloody fool."

Quimbly held the girl's shoulder. She'd pulled her hair back in a white ribbon, and she wore a brandy-colored dress he'd never seen before. She'd washed her face and fashioned a necklace for herself from bits of broken dishware.

She smiled, not at all afraid. In fact, as Quimbly looked at her, she leaned into his arm, unfolding her fingers to reveal a stolen bracelet. Curing this girl of her memory was not an abuse of power, he decided. The Fool would not mind, would never know. She couldn't be part of the River Gang, no matter how good a thief she became. Besides, he wouldn't be thieving much longer himself. Quimbly reached into his pocket, swung the watch before her eyes as he'd been taught.

"Let me lead you," he said, the words less important than their sound. Morning light colored the sky: apricot, silver, and green — the thousand shades of her eyes. "Let me tell you a story."

The words poured from his lips as Parkhurst and the

others dragged the pig iron onto the rocks. "Come on," they called. "Give us a hand." But Quimbly ignored them, and he didn't follow when they left for the docks in search of bulging purses and wallets. Animal magnetism was not something he could control, he realized. It flowed through him, his force, the girl's. It collected like gulls around an old carcass, a flock that might lift from the ground any moment and soar. "Come with me," he said. He'd evoked the Fool's magic. The sun felt hot on his skin. "Come with me."

She clutched his fingers, and together they ran, past the turn where the Fool waited, past Parkhurst and Phineas and Cobb and the docks, and the markets and lumbering trains. And Quimbly raised his free hand to the sky, toward the celestial bodies he knew were pulling him, him and the girl, through the fluid of life.

#

N aked, Edwin Macready's legs and lower abdomen quivered. His feet and ankles paled to an unsightly yellow; his chest, cruelly carved by his disease, curved as delicate as a china bowl. He folded his hands over his genitals. A sulphurous smell of sparks, long extinguished, filled the air.

"Bit of good news today," he said, blue eyes gazing longingly to the left of Doctor Steenwycks's shoulder, where a woolen vest and underpants lay exposed on the examination table.

Doctor Benjamin Steenwycks, who had just finished implanting a fist-sized copper electrode in a damp sponge, raised the instrument to the gaslight to observe his work. Behind him coils of wire and sharp-toothed gears hung from hooks on the wall. Scattered hammers, glass jars of odd nails and screws, and fragments of welded metal gave the small office the feel of a clock repair shop. "Yes?" he said.

"I've been promoted to head clerk."

"Wonderful news! And you're feeling—" The doctor nodded toward Edwin's groin.

"Better," Edwin said, suddenly remorseful. The truth of the matter, as any clerk knew well, was that "head clerk" meant little more than undesired responsibility and additional unpaid hours. No matter how long or hard he worked at the undergarment department at Macy's, he would never afford Doctor Steenwycks's fees. Edwin stood in the scratched copper treatment dish only because the doctor studied neurasthenia in the lower middle class: single men, who paid eight dollars a month to live in dingy boarding-houses, who worked late into the night at factories that rose like flaming candles throughout New York.

Neurasthenia, the doctor claimed, was prevalent among the poor and rich alike, though it was more often diagnosed among the latter. In fact, ailing nerves were the root of all human misery. What but disease could explain the conditions the destitute chose for themselves?

Doctor Steenwycks diagnosed and cured more cases of nerves than any other doctor. He was highly regarded in the medical community. Other doctors as well as patients consulted him on every medical matter: the use of carbolic acid in surgery, the relationship of clean water to public health, the best treatment for cysts, the repair of fistulas. A man of vast means, descendant from a long succession of brilliant doctors, he worked because passion drove him. And one day, after his cousin Letty died and he inherited the family estate, which would have been his had his father not been such a fool, he would move his practice from the lower floor of his Eighteenth Street brownstone to Orchard Street, his ancestral home, which had four chimneys and a rich history of success. When he spoke of it, the doctor looked very wise, his eyes magnified behind spectacles, his hair a neat coif of brown curls.

"Cure the body, the rest will follow," he said.

Edwin nodded. The clerk received free treatments, generously scheduled for dawn so that he could depart in time to begin his twelve-hour day, but he was often too tired to follow conversation. Beneath his feet the metal dish felt cold. The thought of failure troubled him as it had each morning since the doctor began treatments three weeks earlier. What if he never again felt the healing shock? What if Doctor Steenwycks turned him out of the clinic before Edwin owned his own shop, like the butcher's assistant the doctor had cured in only four sessions? Or the waiter who now owned a stagecoach and lived in a brownstone on St. Nicholas Avenue?

"You're responding," the doctor said. A set of pliers

bulged from the slit pocket of his tweed jacket. "The higher doses of current are helping." He consulted a leather-bound journal, scribbled a quick calculation, and struck a rectangular gong, which rang with a resounding clatter. "Herbert!" he called. "The magneto!"

Herbert, the doctor's diminutive assistant, responded to the summons before the gong ceased to sound. Never once taking his rust brown eyes from Edwin's thin, naked frame, he bowed slightly and stepped forward to grasp the crank handle of the cabinet-sized cylindrical machine. Nickel-plated bars gleamed beside coils that spiraled into the dark core of the device, the place where the current came from, at least so Edwin believed, when the smooth metal cylinder spun. With exaggerated effort, Herbert turned the machine's L-shaped handle. The exposed iron frame trembled to the hum of spinning gears and the clunk of an improperly aligned screw. Doctor Steenwycks, wires trailing from each hand, raised his electrodes.

"Have you spoken to that girl?" he asked.

Edwin's interest in a lady had been the first sign of recovery. And ever since he'd mentioned the short-haired girl, whom he'd first seen on the street outside Macy's, the doctor had asked after her.

"You must speak with her." Doctor Steenwycks ran the electrode over Edwin's left thigh, and the muscles twitched violently. "You mustn't let your nerves interfere."

Herbert cranked the magneto rapidly. The odd clunk blurred into the hum of the gears. Again the current shot through Edwin, this time near his abdomen. Shock pounded his flesh. His skin flushed, his breath came in quick bursts. He set his teeth against the pain that coursed through his body. Sweat hung in the air, filling the small office with its rich scent.

EDWIN BRUSHED BY the two uniformed policemen who guided the stream of ladies to and from the front doors of Macy's. The clock struck eight, and he decided to forgo breakfast and begin work (his first day as head clerk of the ladies' undergarment department) a half hour early. All of New York was his, he thought as he passed the plate glass windows surrounded by early-morning shoppers. He would rise through society's ranks as gracefully as the moon rose through the night sky. Startled, he realized that he had begun to whistle. He paused, looked about to see if anyone had noticed. Shoppers thronged: skirts, parcels, flat-toed shoes on sooty cobblestone. The day had warmed, contrary to rumors of a strong coastal storm. And there, right before him, was the girl.

Hatless, as usual, she walked with a purposeful stride. She wore her skirt shorter than respectable women — her ankles flashed where the hem grazed the top of her shoes. She carried a pair of long white gloves, as if she'd been too busy to pull them on, and slung over one shoulder her leather bag bulged with books and papers. Most mornings, she walked on the north side of Fourteenth Street, and Edwin would watch her through the glass of the small coffeehouse, where he sat over coffee and toast. Today she'd chosen the south side, and had Edwin not stepped aside, she would have walked right into him. She must be drawn by his energy. Healthy people, successful people, attracted admirers.

"Good morning," he said. The words felt good on his lips.

She stared back at him with inquiring blue eyes. "Do I know you?"

"Well, no." Even as he soared on the morning's infusion of energy, Edwin recognized the first symptoms of his disease descend. His heart beat rapidly, his voice warbled, his palms began to sweat. Had he pushed himself too far? Should he have waited for a few more sessions before addressing her? Confidence was most easily enjoyed alone.

"And you are?" She smiled, radiant as ever, and he imagined the fine string of pearls he would one day wrap around her neck.

"Edwin Macready." Remembering his blue clerk suit, he felt suddenly self-conscious. Did she think he was trying to sell perfume? Toiletries? For a moment, he feared anxiety would paralyze him, drawing the encounter to a close. But then he felt a sensation he hadn't enjoyed in many months: a quickening in his groin. He could not fail now. Not after the treatment. "I've been promoted to head clerk."

She nodded, fussed with her bag — perhaps searching for a calling card. Edwin watched, the warmth spreading up through his chest, his neck, his cheeks. He hadn't blushed so deeply in years.

"I'm running for Congress," she said at last, handing him a pamphlet.

"Why —" Edwin folded the paper twice before he realized he'd nearly destroyed the likeness of Madeline Cady that covered a full third of the sheet. How could someone so lovely speak such nonsense? "But you can't vote."

"Not right, is it?" She shook her head. Behind her a carriage pushed between the crowd of shoppers and a dead horse, left for the sanitation department in front of Oscar's Tavern. A child, clad only in an ash-colored undershirt, screamed as a woman struck him, and dozens of blue-clad clerks rushed to their shifts. The boardinghouses, dingy dens without fire escapes or ventilation, now stood empty.

"The law —" Edwin tried to collect his thoughts, but he rarely held forth on matters of politics, his days filled with the latest colors and cuts and bargains, and he could only gesture his argument.

"The law says nothing about *running* for office."

"Who'd —" He watched her, her lips slightly apart, the

morning light lending its softness to her skin. "Who would *vote* for you?"

"You're a clerk. Would you rather fight for an eight-hour workday? Or new water pipes for the mansions on the East Side? You're the one who'll vote for me. You and people like you — people tired of sleeping on the counters at work because they lack the energy to return home at the end of the day."

Edwin, who had (before his treatment began) often slept on the bench behind the jewelry department, his shirt folded neatly beside him so that he might appear fresh in the morning, imagined Madeline slipping into Macy's late at night. Was it possible that she'd seen him asleep at work?

"Can I count on your vote?"

The nonsense Madeline spoke gave him confidence. "Will you have dinner with me tonight?"

She regarded him, her lips curled in a half smile. "If you'll vote for me," she said, extending her hand to take his, just as a gentleman might.

AFTER ELEVEN HOURS in the undergarment department, the effects of the morning's treatment waned. He'd pushed himself to the limit, after all, speaking to Madeline and then shouldering the new responsibilities of head clerk. His former colleagues had not taken well to his promotion, refusing to acknowledge first his polite and later his barked commands, and the tables of stockings and undershirts stood in disarray. All the difficult clients now fell to him as well. In one shift, he'd addressed Miss Poppenhusen's faulty garter, Mrs. Matsell's missized breast-heaver, and Mrs. Gloria Howlett's lopsided corset. He wore the gloom of his profession like protective armor, but the incessant demands invariably passed through. Even the prospect of his date with Madeline brought little comfort. Would that he could return to Doctor Steenwyck's clinic for an infusion of energy before the event!

"Clerk?"

Edwin's teeth hurt as he ground them: Mrs. Fuller and Mrs. Plunkett, both renowned patrons of the shops along the Sixth Avenue ladies' mile, had arrived, and he must help them, for who but head clerk could properly advise them? Mrs. Fuller, hair pulled back and smoothed into a large chignon, refused to accept her great girth, and clerks were forever retagging the larger sizes as popular mediums before presenting them to her. She was famous for ordering gowns from abroad, which she always spoke of but never wore. Her old friend, Mrs. Plunkett, more graceful in stature, had sharp, birdlike features, complete with a narrow pointed nose.

"May I help you?"

"All of New York is talking about the Grand Duke,"

Mrs. Fuller said, one great arm thrown over her head. "Grand Duke, Grand Duke, Grand Duke."

The great dame obviously required an appropriate outfit for tomorrow night's ball in the Grand Duke's honor. Edwin had helped over a dozen fine ladies secure undergarments for their new gowns.

"You will need the perfect bustle," Edwin said.

"And so I shall."

Edwin attempted a courteous smile, but managed only a grimace, a look that the women might well have mistaken for contempt. "You'll likely want the horsehair."

He led the two ladies to the front table where the fashionable false bums were prominently displayed. Sized to add between twelve and twenty-four inches of depth to a woman's hindquarters, the garments stood on a yard of cream-colored silk beside a set of tortoiseshell combs and several false hairpieces designed to add volume to the back of the head as well.

"Last season's bustles contain stiffened gauze." Edwin turned the inferior garment to display the buckles. "Not nearly as firm as the —"

"As the horse. I see," Mrs. Fuller said. "What do you think?" She turned to Mrs. Plunkett, who laughed as if the thought of the giant undergarment embarrassed her. "Could we?"

Edwin stepped aside so the women could more intimately

consider the garments. Such waiting always made him feel alone, outcast, aware of the fact that they and not he attended these balls and could afford to spend two months salary (his salary) on a single hardened mass of fibers. The electrical shock treatment may have helped him, may have raised his spirits enough that he easily stood out among his colleagues, but Dr. Steenwycks had not cured Edwin. His life was still confined to the single room he let at half cost as it fronted the elevated train track along Ninth Avenue. His window, dark with soot, hardly protected him from the thundering steam engines. Was it his fault that he was born into poverty? That his father died of a diseased heart, leaving his mother to support three children on a seamstress salary? Would he ever wear anything but the stiff clerk's uniform? Fear commanded his fingers, which found comfort between his teeth, his gnawed cuticles bleeding.

"Clerk," Mrs. Fuller demanded. She had wrapped the horsehair bustle around her skirt and both she and Mrs. Plunkett now struggled with the rash of straps and buckles. Another step backward and the two would topple the vanity table, covered with glass bottles of scents and powders. He should stop them. But Edwin could not free himself from the crushing grip of his disease. To him, the table had already tipped over. The women had reported him, the negligent clerk, to the store manager. Stripped of his uniform, he sat destitute on the street.

"Balance," Edwin whispered.

Mrs. Fuller leaned forward, her breath short and her bosom struggling to emerge from the prison of her neckline. "What was that?" she said.

"Balance." Edwin spoke more loudly this time, the morning's confidence returning to him.

"Well, yes," Mrs. Fuller said. "I suppose."

Mrs. Plunkett released her hold on the bustle, which fell to the floor with a crack. "Have you any others?" she said. "Of the horse?"

"Let me check the storeroom." Edwin backed away, hoping that in the darkness, surrounded by crates of whites and stockings, he could find a moment's respite. Aside from his colleagues, swarthy men who now hid behind stacks of undershirts pretending to fold, the floor was empty.

He was nearly to the storeroom's curtained doorway when he encountered a creature, just four feet tall in cloth slippers and a full flounced skirt. It regarded him with eyes obscured by thick wiry brows. Hair covered its cheeks and chin, forming a beard that hung well below what appeared to be a tremendous bosom. And though the monstrous being wore stockings and fitted sleeves, the cloth rose over what could only be clumps of body hair, long and, judging from what Edwin observed on the hands, dark as a bear's coat. Perhaps sensing his disgust, the figure pulled a scarf over its face.

"May I help you?" he managed, though he could not imagine the creature in any of the fine silk garments he carried. Her clothes were of impeccable quality, tailored to fit the odd lines of her form, but not of a fashion Macy's carried. Startled, he noticed a wedding band around her left ring finger.

"A bustle," she said, "for the Grand Duke's ball."

"A bustle?" For a moment, Edwin could not remember where the garments were stored, or the two clients, Mrs. Fuller and Mrs. Plunkett, he'd left beside the display table.

"If you'd be so kind as to wait — " He couldn't bring such a customer before the fine ladies.

"If you'd direct me." She released the scarf, her fingers thick and clumsy and in need of a good pair of gloves. "I have a show in an hour."

Edwin tried to imagine her parents. How horrified they must have been, unless, of course, they shared her aspect. "You must have — "

"The circus," she said. "I dance for the sideshow. Or at balls, for entertainment. I know how you see me." She ran her fingers through the hair on her cheeks.

"Yes," Edwin said. As ugly as the creature was, he felt compassion for her, a flood of sympathy that forced him to step forward, to guide her by the shoulder. "Come this way."

◆ ◆ ◆

MRS. FULLER HAD unfastened the gauze bustle, which lay like a corpse beside the horsehair one, when Edwin and the beast-woman approached the table. The large woman had obviously hurt herself, and Mrs. Plunkett was dutifully bent over her friend, massaging her shoulders with quick circular strokes. Upon seeing the creature, however, Mrs. Fuller's injury appeared to vanish.

"Why, my dear!" she cried, hastening to meet the apelike woman and extending a hand in greeting. "What an unexpected pleasure."

Edwin, braced for a confrontation, watched in amazement as both Mrs. Fuller and Mrs. Plunkett fluttered around his new client.

"Doctor Steenwycks announced that you are a new species! Can you imagine? And you speak so well, my dear. And dance." Mrs. Fuller turned to her friend. "Have you seen Mistress Gradiva dance?"

"Not yet," Mrs. Plunkett admitted.

"Well, she's marvelous." Mrs. Fuller's smile, as wide and round as her cheeks, nearly made her face pretty, childish good looks, disturbing on her large form. "Will you dance for us, darling. Just for a moment?"

"Here?" Mistress Gradiva noted the narrow stretch of tiled floor, the tables and glass casings. "Without music?"

"Come, come. I'll sing." Before Mistress Gradiva could

reply, Mrs. Fuller began, her voice rising sharply. "Singing, the reapers homeward come, Io! Io!"

Mistress Gradiva bowed her head and stepped with surprising grace to the left.

"Merrily singing the harvest home, Io! Io!"

Edwin slipped back, unable to hide between the hanging garters, but desiring nothing more. He was not a well man, couldn't they see? Reserve their antics for the hours he did not work? Mrs. Fuller had begun to clap, her arms swinging to the rhythm of her song. Mrs. Plunkett, who had initially tried to sing along, hummed a different melody, as Mistress Gradiva danced, her clothes pulling over her form like the half-shed skin of a snake. Each time she raised her arms, the dress pulled higher and tighter over her fur, and soon, Edwin was certain, it would pull away altogether.

"With cheerful song, Io! Io!"

He imagined Dr. Steenwycks's office, the pleasure and pain of his daily shock, the tear in his muscles. He closed his eyes. Inside, he had energy. He would survive this shift. He would—

"Leave the poor woman alone." Madeline's voice. Edwin opened his eyes in time to see her frown. She now wore a scarlet dress and a cropped waistcoat cut for a man.

"Madeline!" He'd had no time to prepare for her arrival,

had not even realized that his shift had ended, that the time of their arranged meeting had come.

"Madeline Cady," Mrs. Fuller said, her song left abruptly unfinished. Mistress Gradiva finished a spin and stood with heels pressed together, toes pointed out. "It's true, then, what I hear?"

"I cannot imagine what you hear," Madeline said. "I prefer not to."

"There's no need for rudeness," Mrs. Plunkett said. "We were merely enjoying —"

"Dear, dear," Mrs. Fuller said. "You're as abrasive as they say."

"And you are?" Madeline said.

"Gloria Fuller." A brusque nod introduced the large woman's next observation. "We think you're taking this all a little too far."

"Taking what?" Madeline nodded to Edwin in greeting. He blushed, tried to smile, felt his face tighten. Though used to women, particularly of Mrs. Fuller's sort, he felt powerless.

"This matter of voting."

Mrs. Plunkett nodded vehemently. "It's not ladylike."

"I'm afraid you're unable to vote against me," Madeline said. "Which is a pity as I have quite a bit of support. Haven't I, Edwin?"

Edwin nodded, unable to conjure appropriate words.

He'd hoped to disabuse the fair Madeline of this very craziness over an inexpensive candlelit dinner. But speaking these plans seemed ill advised. Mistress Gradiva tugged at his shirtsleeve, the broken horsehair bustle hanging from her fingertips.

"I'd like this wrapped," she said. "For the ball."

"Ah! The ball!" Mrs. Plunkett clapped her hands, delighted, and with a glare toward Madeline continued, "I'll see the *remainder* of the performance then."

"Perhaps we'll meet there," Madeline said, "should I be so fortunate as to see you again."

"The ball?" Edwin could not hide his amazement. Was all of New York invited to the Grand Duke's ball? Was he alone denied access to the finery?

"Yes, the ball," Madeline said, lips forming a wry smile.

Blown-glass lamps, red, green, and blue, lit the Bowery. Edwin led Madeline by the arm, his elbow awkward where it touched her torso. The clouds threatened rain, but revelers still filled the street. Germans, dressed in lederhosen and suspenders, played discordant waltzes on trumpets, tubas, worn fiddles. Street merchants hawked hot corn. The air smelled of horse urine and fried oysters, and the streets held the slick, wet chill of the coming rains.

"Do you frequent these parts?" Madeline asked. Though she stood near, she did not look at him. He followed her gaze to the parading couples, young, mostly, spirited, light as their laugher. She did not join their merriment, but she seemed amused by it.

"No," Edwin said. He'd heard the other clerks speak fondly of the Bowery but had himself never ventured out to the street before. It was louder than he'd expected. Far more crowded, and not at all romantic. Right now, he stood beside a pasty drunk, who sang, sometimes to the music, sometimes to songs that played inside his head. A whore, bodice only half fastened, rushed past on her way to a darker, less-traveled alley. "I thought — "

"It's lovely," she said. "The true New York. The New York of honest people, with honest lives and work and predicaments. Look at them all. Just look."

Edwin considered the crowd, wary of the circle of dancers he'd noticed grabbing reluctant bystanders. "I suppose," he said. When he imagined his life with Madeline, this street played no role. He and Madeline would live far uptown, and he would read both the morning and evening papers and hire a host of servants to help his dear wife run the house. They would take tea in the afternoon and brandy with their evening meal. He'd have no less than six horses draw their carriage, and he'd buy fine dresses from Worth, in Paris.

"These are my people." She pulled a handful of pamphlets from beneath her jacket.

A butcher, still clad in a blood-splattered apron passed near, and Madeline stepped toward him. "Shorter work days!" she called. "Higher wages!"

Edwin watched, dumbstruck. How could she proselytize here? Now? She was his for the evening. In earlier days, in days before he'd found inner strength, he might have stood silently beside her, shrinking from the passing leers. He pulled Madeline to the side of the road, where a covered doorway provided some privacy. "You can't do that," he said.

A pamphlet, soaked by the night humidity, hung limply in Madeline's hand. She gazed steadily at Edwin, wide-spaced eyes inquisitive. "Are you deranged?" she asked at last.

"Deranged?" For a moment, Edwin thought he might vomit. But he would not allow his nerves to defy him. His voice would not shake, his hands would not tremble.

"You promised your support this morning," she said.

"Not this. I didn't promise this." Beside Edwin, two drunks began to brawl. A thrown metal flask crashed against the cobblestone. Edwin's lips jerked open, his hand grasped her soft arm. "You don't belong here, doing this. You belong at home with children, a loving husband . . ."

A great torrent of rain tore through the sky. The music stopped, the dancing halted. Running bodies filled the broad street.

"Don't ever speak to a woman that way." Madeline glared

at him, her features pinched with distaste. "In fact, don't speak to me at all." She turned, stepped away, her shoulders rigid.

"Wait!" Edwin followed. "I only — "

"If you come near me, I'll call for a constable."

"I — "

"Constable!" she cried, raising a drenched arm into the driving rain.

Edwin stopped, uncertain. Would an officer listen to him, a clerk, over a woman invited to the Grand Duke's ball? Likely not, and there was no telling what Madeline might say. She was the one deranged, not he, though his passion for her remained.

"You must not walk the streets alone!" Edwin cried after her, but his voice held no strength. Water beaded in his hair, flowed down the sides of his face. His evening had only just begun. He hadn't even taken her to dinner.

Stunned, he followed a crowd of street revelers — young men who moved like their laughter, in bursts interrupted with wild boasts and confident wagers — through a wide doorway. Absently, he handed the ticket booth a nickel and passed into a grand hall lit with brilliant torches. Flickering shadows colored the room in formless blue-gray swatches; the muffled sound of pouring rain dulled the audience's applause. Hundreds of occupied seats faced a central stage, which stretched long and flat in an oval. An organ grinder played, but Edwin didn't hear the music, didn't even realize that he blocked a young girl's view of the stage, till her mother rapped his shoulder.

"I'm sorry," he said.

Onstage, a lace-clad woman stood on the bare back of a white stallion. Feathers and glittering jewels. A hunchback stood center stage calling out tricks: "Jump!" or "Spin!" which the woman performed. Clowns with white faces and lurid red smiles strolled among the seats with candied apples, which they offered to children and then pulled away. *For me! All for me!* they seemed to cry. To one side stood a midget dressed as a leprechaun, an obese woman in a tremendous silk dress, a man with an extra arm, an albino whose pale skin seemed to shimmer, identical twins dressed in matching striped trousers, and Mistress Gradiva, who danced just as she had in the department store, except that she now wore a short-sleeved gold dress and no stockings so as to reveal the hair on her arms and legs. She spun, kicked, raised her arms above her head. Then she reached toward a large wooden crate, which exploded as a bald man in a bright blue suit jumped out. He bowed to the audience, took the mistress's hand, and together the two waltzed.

Edwin watched, though his thoughts were far from the parading grotesques. Cold, despite the heat of the crowd and the flaming torches, he waited only for the rain to subside so that he might return alone to his squalid apartment.

The first inklings of a plan had begun to take form in his head. He would see Madeline again, tomorrow night. He'd hold her, dance with her, sweep her off her feet. And in the morning, to prepare, he would become confident beneath the healing shock of Doctor Steenwycks's magneto.

BENEATH THE LOW ceiling of the doctor's office, Edwin's muscles twitched in violent spasms. The current built inside him, hot as burning oil: pure energy, intoxicating. He raised his arms as the electrodes passed over his forehead, his chest. Doctor Steenwycks's fingers and the damp sponge encasing the metal disks had no weight on his skin. Only the current touched him. Eyes shut, Edwin could see it: a tidal wave of orange and red. "Yes!" he cried. The force had never been so strong, so constant. The howl of the magneto rose, piercing and high, louder than even a moment before. Exploding. Only after the shock ceased, did Edwin recognize the cadence of his screams. "Very good," Doctor Steenwycks told him. "Very good."

THE EVENING OF the Grand Duke's ball found Edwin in high spirits. Without any trouble, he'd smuggled a smartly cut tailcoat, fitted trousers, and a pair of fine leather boots from Macy's. And he had only to shave and trim his hanging cuticles without drawing blood before he set off for the dance. The fact that he did not have an invitation no longer deterred him.

He left his carriage-sized room, his cast-off clerk's garb strewn over the floor, and walked barefoot up Broadway — a plan he'd devised to preserve the soles of his shoes so that he might return them to Macy's shelves unharmed. The night stretched hot and humid. Sweat collected in the fabric of his shirt and threatened to stain the fine weave of his borrowed outer garments. But Edwin felt calm. Madeline could not resist, would not resist his request for a dance, and he'd win her subtly, avoiding her mad politics till she hung limply in his arms and agreed to abandon her notions forever.

A dozen fine carriages stood before the music hall, each with a driver dressed nearly as well as Edwin. Women in tremendous skirts required two or three gentlemen escorts before they could travel the yards between their coaches and the hall's grand entryway. Edwin slipped into the shadows and tied his boots, his eyes adjusting to the landscape of wealth. He must remember to approach with confidence.

"Why, Edwin Macready! Such an unexpected pleasure." Strolling through the shadows was none other than Doctor Steenwycks, his hair soaped back, and his suit impeccably clean. "I came out for air," he explained. "Have you met everybody?"

"I've only just arrived," Edwin said, deciding that anything more might sound suspicious.

"It's good to see you feeling so well!" The doctor threw a welcoming arm around his shoulder and led him up the marble steps to where a cluster of gentlemen stood. Doctor Steenwycks made introductions, turning first to a stooped, bearded fellow in a towering hat.

"Another patient of yours!" the man said. "The last made such a fine manager." He extended his hand, the skin as soft as worn fabric. "You're not seeking employment, are you?"

Edwin turned to the doctor, unsure of how to respond. Was the man hiring him? Here on the steps of the Grand Duke's ball?

"Edwin's a wonderful worker," Doctor Steenwycks said. "A fine man all around now that he's cured."

"I'd expect nothing less from one of your patients." The man peered into Edwin's half-open mouth, perhaps counting the teeth, or confirming their quality. "Karl Harrison," he said at last, "at your service."

Edwin looked past him, to the far side of the street where a familiar voice cried out. "Shorter work days! Higher pay!" Madeline stood behind a small table, her short hair framing her lovely features. She wore her day clothes, a gray skirt with matching blouse and only a ribbon for jewelry. No one stopped to take her fliers; no one listened, though several young men pointed to her and laughed.

"She's been at it for hours," Harrison said, shaking his head and turning to join the party.

"Why spoil the evening?" Doctor Steenwycks agreed. "Come along, Edwin. The show's begun."

Edwin stood at the doorstep. Inside, well-dressed women paraded over parquet floors. The light played over bodies, grown wider and taller with the clothes Edwin sold, the female form, distorted by garments, was no longer human, though none of the gentlemen seemed to mind. At the center, upon a raised platform, Mistress Gradiva danced, hairy arms and legs bared for the spectators, fur twitching as she spun. The hunchback had come as well, Edwin realized, along with the midget who now carried a miniature parasol.

"Come along, Edwin," the doctor repeated.

"Why can't we vote? Why can't women vote?" Madeline called. Edwin couldn't bring her inside dressed as she was. He couldn't dance with her now that she'd upset the guests with her foolishness. But he could slip out of the party and talk to her later. He could leave the ball to help her, make her come to her senses. Or he could find her tomorrow, he decided, on Fourteenth Street. He'd share news of his profession: a manager, for Karl Harrison. He'd point to himself, a healed man, a man who required a respectable wife. He'd offer an ultimatum: me or the vote. She would make the right decision. And with one step, Edwin entered the celebration.

❧ THE SIBLINGS ❧

When the snow had gone but winter had not yet lifted, Abraham returned to New York. He'd left the city as a slight, dark-haired youth, a boy who made promises like a man: "I'll cure you," to his mad sister, Lillian; "I'll write every Sunday," to his older sister, Chastity; "I'll marry you," to Hilda, the judge's daughter; "I'll take over your practice," to his father, who had no intention of passing on any time soon, God rest his soul. He returned from abroad, after squandering the family fortune on ill-fated bets, with a holy kind of pallor. He wore his hair long on top and slicked back in what was likely the latest Swiss fashion, and he squinted through a pair of eyeglasses engraved with his initials so that anyone meeting his eye was distracted by the curve of the letters cut into the glass.

His ship took twenty-one days to arrive in New York, allowing his father's patients to learn of Abraham's return before the boy set foot in Manhattan. People speculated whether the elder Doctor Steenwycks would disown the boy, or if Hilda, the judge's daughter, would still consent to marry him. Since most of Doctor Benjamin Steenwycks's patients lived in the area and frequented the same barbers and restaurants, even healthy people began to have opinions about what might transpire between their doctor and his son, which is why John's Saloon, which served exclusively cider and tea, was standing room only the day Abraham's ship arrived.

The bar was dingy and cold, and the tables shook whenever John picked up or set down a glass, but the pub's two picture windows faced the Steenwyckses' brownstone on Eighteenth Street and afforded the best view on the street. Nearly fifty people saw blind old Miss Harding race onto the street with her blouse on inside out and her hair undone and falling round her shoulders so that even those who weren't given to imagination could tell that she'd once been quite attractive.

"He's dead! He's dead!" she wailed.

A dozen people raced out to the brownstone-lined street to help her, because although she was blind and not well liked, she wasn't crazy, like Lillian Steenwycks, and if she said someone was dead, someone most certainly was.

"Come here, out of the street," Hilda said. The judge's girl had been in John's Saloon since eight that morning. She'd painted her lips a pretty red and wore the family pearls in her ears, the ones saved for special occasions. Her shoes were new and tight and no one thought she could run in them. But she reached Miss Harding first and led the blind woman away from the street where automobiles sometimes sped by at such reckless speeds that the neighborhood agreed the machines were the devil's own invention.

"What happened? Who's dead?" John spat out his chewing tobacco — a habit everyone forgave him for because his nature was kind and pleasant — and set down the tea cup he'd been drying. As the proprietor, he took charge while the others, mostly older folks in pinned hats and black garb, owing to mourning, pressed close to hear at least a few words.

"Doctor Steenwycks," Miss Harding said.

Mrs. Chadwick, who read cards for a living and was used to jumping to conclusions, raised her arms above the crowd and called out. "He's killed him! Killed his own son!"

"Quiet!" John said and, turning to Miss Harding, asked, "Have you seen the body?"

"Seen it? Seen it?" the blind woman asked. "I was with him when he died."

"Tell us everything. Everything, from the beginning."

Miss Harding began to cry, her lids shut fast and the

tears appearing to push through skin. "I loved him," she said. "I adored him."

"He's been away for so long — " John began, before a realization corroborated by the blind woman's state of undress made him catch his breath. "Doctor Benjamin Steenwycks? Were you with Doctor Benjamin Steenwycks?"

"Dead! He's dead. Died in my arms."

Were it not for the fact that the good doctor was dead, the excitement over the discovery of his romantic liaison might have drowned out the blind woman's testimony. As it was, those gathered swallowed the revelation like a large chunk of stewed beef.

"Have the police been notified?" John asked. "Have you notified the police?"

"How horrible!" cried Miss Stein, known for feeding every feral cat and dog in the neighborhood.

Others began to comment as well: "And he never laid eyes on his son," and "It's for the best, poor, dear man," and "God moves in mysterious ways."

THE STEENWYCKSES' BROWNSTONE, a three-story structure in which the doctor had lived and practiced for decades, despite his promise to move to the family estate on Orchard Street (a property he coveted but never inherited), at once became a center of activity, with neighbors arriving every few hours with baked hams, loaves of fresh bread, apple pies, scones, flowers, melons, and, for the young surgeon, a bottle of brandy. The eldest sister, Chastity, presided over each visit with a sad smile and a formality that made everyone uncomfortable and quick to leave despite the unusual circumstances of Doctor Benjamin's death, the newly arrived Abraham, and the mad sister, Lillian, who had always been a source of neighborhood interest.

Chastity, who had her father's firm chin and oddly sloped forehead, appeared withdrawn and noble in a black wool skirt and jacket, which was a little short in the sleeves. She wore her hair in a low bun, and as usual, she'd pulled and fussed with so many pins that not one strand of hair fell over her face where it might have softened her features. Over the course of the ten years that she assisted her father, she witnessed half the block in nothing but smallclothes, leading the majority of patients to dislike and avoid her. She was the only Steenwycks receiving visitors, and therefore an obstacle between the guests and the upper floors, where her more interesting siblings were mourning. Whispered rumors that she was not only severe but also unmoved by her father's passing began to circulate.

Only those who arrived in the late afternoon overheard the cries of the mad sister, Lillian. The family had built a special room for the girl on the top floor, where she spent long hours at the one small window singing and gazing at wrought iron railings, well-tended window boxes, maple trees, and scrawny mutts stretched out on the sidewalk. She never noticed the pairs of old women pointing to her from the street and exchanging quick whispers, or the influx of immigrants and luxury-line passengers who began arriving the day Chelsea Piers opened. The pedestrian traffic enraged the neighbors, who complained of noise and inappropriate dress, though they were mostly interested in themselves: in the fact that Mrs. Chadwick sometimes walked in her sleep or that John's eldest daughter had run off with a drunk or that Hilda had colored her lips a shade too bright.

Lillian herself had lost her color: hair gray and brittle as fish bone, her loose gown white, her cheeks and lips a single shade, pale as the fingernails she refused to have cut. Miss Stein had seen Lillian once and reported that the girl's nails curved round like spirals, so long and heavy she couldn't lift her hands. "That's how they restrain her," she said, unable to explain, when asked, how the madwoman found her way down two flights of stairs to the doctor's office.

Usually the pillows on the walls and floor muffled Lillian's cries, but Abraham, who had arrived home only hours after his father passed away, had led the girl to the family parlor, where he attempted to explain that Father had died and would no longer bring her chocolates. In fact, Doctor Benjamin had long ago ceased bringing sweets, believing that they excited his daughter and made her more violent. But Abraham hadn't consulted Chastity before speaking and had no way of knowing either this or the fact that over the ten years he'd been gone, Lillian had grown to detest slow, comforting words and smiles. She became increasingly nervous as Abraham attempted to calm her, and at last she rushed at her brother. Surprised, he fell to the floor, where he suffered the disgrace of calling to Chastity for help. He did not like to depend upon others. Even as a child, he'd preferred to run about with his laces trailing, unwilling to admit that he could not tie them himself.

Chastity excused herself from Mrs. Landers to race upstairs. And though the guest had arrived with a pudding and a tin of fudge, she had to show herself to the door.

"Lillian, stop." Chastity took Lillian's hand and pulled her up, careful that the girl's feet did not strike the clawed couch leg or the cabinet containing the few remaining pieces of the good china. Her father's French novel lay overturned on the floor along with a spilled glass of brandy dropped in the scuffle.

The madwoman spat. She'd been close to her father, or at least, she appeared to have been, as she often followed him as if she were a pale puff of a duckling and he a feathered ass. The Steenwycks siblings were close as well: Abraham had indeed written Chastity every Sunday for the past ten years, and Chastity had kept her brother's gambling debts hidden from her father, her loyalty remaining with her sibling and her belief that he would make good his promise to win back the fortune.

"She's far worse than when I left," Abraham observed from the floor.

"She's excited," Chastity said.

"Does she often attack people?" A thin red line cut across Abraham's upper lip. He dabbed the blood with a hand-kerchief he kept in the breast pocket of his suit coat. His luggage had not yet arrived from the port, but he'd shaved with his father's old kit and combed his hair neatly. He re-garded Chastity through his initialed spectacles. "I worked with violent patients in Switzerland, as you know. I have acquired a great deal of expertise regarding them."

"She's rarely violent."

"She's certainly not sane." Abraham pushed back the cuff of his left sleeve, revealing a crescent of soft pink scar tissue. "A garden shovel," he explained, "in the hands of one of Doctor Gottlieb Burckhardt's patients. I've been marked for life — but it was well worth it. Now the patient is fully docile. The last time I showed him my arm, he ran his fin-gers over the scar with absolute tenderness."

"Father and I . . ." Chastity's voice faltered a bit as she spoke. "We've been instructing her in art and music. If you saw her watercolors."

Lillian's paintings hung all over the doctor's office: bright green landscapes, each with a dog or two — usually a large, mangy mutt. She described light with spirals of color and never concerned herself with shadow, so that each image had a haunting quality, a flatness, a sort of impossibility.

"She lives in a prison," Abraham said.

Lillian opened her mouth and silently scraped the dirt from the underside of her long, but not spiraling, fingernails. For some moments she stood, lips parted. At last she spoke: "Fly, fly, fly away home."

Abraham shook his head sadly. "I can help her," he said. "I know a surgery—Doctor Gottlieb Burckhardt performed it some half-dozen times. I can show you his papers on it. He removed merely the front part of the brain. Just bits of the frontal lobe, and—"

"Let's go to your room." Chastity, skin blotchy from the tears she wiped away each time a visitor arrived, reached forward to take her sister's hand.

To her brother, she added what her father—who'd read Doctor Gottlieb Burckhardt's papers and knew that two of six of his patients had died—would have said: "You will not experiment on Lillian."

PEOPLE SAID THAT if Doctor Benjamin Steenwycks hadn't died in the throes of ecstasy, his son would never have remained in New York nor performed the Swiss surgery on his sister, and none of the siblings' troubles would have started. Even clear-thinking folks like Mr. and Mrs.

Landers who ran the pharmacy said so, folks who knew that the troubles really started not when the doctor died in the arms of blind Miss Harding, but twenty-four years ago, when Lillian was born and it was obvious from her smile and dull green eyes that she was mad. Other troubles followed: the Macy's clerk Doctor Steenwycks killed by accident with his curative magneto, the death of his wife, the loss of his fortune. Mostly people liked to talk about the doctor's death, and only the doctor's death, because they didn't care for Miss Harding, mainly because she asked the neighborhood boys for assistance and never once paid them a cent, and they liked to hold her accountable for all the Steenwyckses' troubles.

After the funeral, attended by well over two hundred of Doctor Benjamin Steenwycks's former patients and colleagues, Abraham took over his father's practice. Nearly every one of his father's old patients came by with complaints of toothaches and ingrown nails in order to get a good look at the boy, now a man, who had gambled away a fortune. Abraham treated each ailment with confidence, diagnosing conditions and prescribing cures before his patients finished relating their symptoms. He was a fine doctor, the clients agreed, better than his father. The opinion spread rapidly and found its way back to Abraham within days. Chastity continued to work as the practice's nurse; Lillian remained in her upstairs quarters, her condition unaltered, for her brother would not perform the surgery for some months yet. She appeared more often in the young doctor's office, and it was rumored he released her from her pillowed room so as to better study her. Once the girl even made her way to the street, where she terrified a pair of stray dogs as she ran after them.

Weeks passed and might have continued to pass in a similar balance were it not for the death of Letty Tucker, the siblings' great aunt, who had lived to eighty-six on a diet of boiled vegetables.

Letty left the siblings the large estate at 62 Orchard Street, which had been in the family for four generations, though Letty occupied it for two, outliving her young cousin and the siblings' father, who had vainly awaited his inheritance. She'd tended to the upkeep of the property herself, which is why the roof had leaks, the walls and floors water stains, the garden paths mangled roots and upturned tiles. The closets contained hundreds of gray larvae that seemed disinclined to become moths; the ground floor reeked of decaying rat and mildew, the curtains faded from blue to off-white; the wallpaper, where it still adhered, appeared more gray than colored. The house had once been used as a phrenology institute, and framed articles cut from obscure medical journals still proclaimed that the bumps and curves of heads could reveal the deep secrets of personality. Now the building stood as the sole single-family residence in a neighborhood of deteriorating tenements.

Chastity had never been moved by physical things before, but she loved the old house the moment she set eyes on it. She felt a sudden and overwhelming content, imagining herself in the garden, the house with fresh cream paint, new roof and chimney — one of the four had fallen, leaving behind only a stump of brick. She had fantasies of roast lamb and buttered potato cooking in the kitchen, the *Moonlight* Sonata playing on the old harpsichord in the sitting room. In her fantasy, a fire warmed the hearth, despite the fact that the property had fallen to the siblings in late July and the heat and humidity nearly prevented her from venturing out to visit 62 Orchard Street at all.

She decided that she and her brother and sister would live there together. They would fit out a whole wing for Lillian, grow squash in the yard, store winter and summer clothing in separate closets. Chastity would cook feasts for her brother, Abraham, whose return had gladdened her heart, despite the horrid circumstances surrounding his arrival and the fact that he no longer confided in her or sought her company. She knew her brother was in love with Hilda, and Chastity suspected herself of petty jealousy.

Weekends and evenings when the practice was closed, Chastity swept and dusted and aired out the house, where she found herself repeating catchy lines from the tunes her mad sister sang, "Fly, fly, fly away home" or "Little bird, little cage, sing, sing, sing." She interviewed construction workers, met a competent one named Joseph Miller. Joseph accepted each of her assignments with a thoughtful nod and even flirted with her, surprising the neighborhood boys who sometimes went down to Orchard Street to spy. Joseph busied himself with the front porch, which had a westerly tilt and had rotted so thoroughly that emaciated cats risked falling through the floorboards. He promised to have it in good shape before winter, when he would carry her over the threshold. Even then, he spoke of marriage. Chastity only reddened and turned away.

On weekends Abraham took Lillian down in a hired car, and he and Chastity would take turns minding her. She loved the dandelions that grew by the front of the porch and the clusters of hard dirt that she extracted from the ground with her fingernails. She began to smile when others smiled, and to remember odd games the three had played when they were children, games both her siblings had forgotten, like who could swing their arms for longest or put their head between their knees and pretend to be underwater. She sat with her head down and her dress immodestly pulled to one side, and she laughed loudly, leaving Abraham certain she'd been poisoned by the summer sun. He took her temperature, frowned, led her to the shade, where she played other games, like writing words with twigs, only she'd never been able to write words and instead made patterns on the ground.

Abraham sat down a few yards away, his shirt collar buttoned despite the torridity, a newspaper spread on the ground beneath him to protect his fine Swiss trousers. The clouded sky didn't blunt the sun's heat, though it did soften the light so that the world looked more like one of Lillian's paintings than a real place with dark shadows.

"Could you help me move the table?" Chastity called from inside.

Abraham often left Lillian on her own, releasing her from her padded room. He thought nothing of leaving her alone in the yard. He moved toward the front door. He'd been thinking of Hilda and his dead father, the fortune he'd squandered. If he hadn't gambled the money, he could have remained in Europe under the tutelage of Doctor Gottlieb Burckhardt. He could be performing psychosurgery instead of practicing common medicine. At the very least, he would be out of the oppressive humidity that made him sweaty and irritable.

He crossed the front porch on the narrow planks Joseph Miller had set down to create a temporary passage, moved the table, an old piece that might have had value save for the circular burns and water stains, and sat down with his back to the smoke-blackened wallpaper. Across the floor, a column of ants marched toward the kitchen.

"Won't it be lovely once we're done?" Chastity said.

"The land will fetch a fine price," he said, a thought he'd not consciously acknowledged until that moment. But the heat had intensified the rotting scent of the walls and floor, and he felt himself, suddenly, to be rotting as well, and his sister had begun to reek of mildew.

"We can't sell it," Chastity said firmly. "It's been in the family for generations."

"It's time we moved on then, high time we moved on."

The two would have argued further, except for the rain, falling forcibly.

Abraham turned to the front porch, where Lillian sought refuge.

"Lillian!" Abraham and Chastity rushed to grab her, only Abraham reached the door first, and so it was he who fell through the boards, and he who was struck by the wailing Lillian, terrified by the thunder and rain. Again and again she struck her brother, the skin of her hands white where she clutched a jagged fragment of hard, bloody wood.

ABRAHAM WAS BEDRIDDEN for eight months, too weak to work. Hilda often came to sit with him, but otherwise the home remained empty and sad, the source of the meanest gossip: how the siblings had fallen on hard times, how Chastity fought with her brother, how mad Lillian was left to starve in the attic.

Chastity oversaw the sale of 62 Orchard Street herself, collecting a tidy sum that felt filthy in her hands. The family had no other source of income, and she knew better than to complain.

Lillian remained locked in her rooms painting pictures of Orchard Street, lovely pictures of old, rotting windows and doors that only made it harder for Chastity to forget the estate that had so briefly resided in her hopes. She brought her sister meals and sometimes sat with her, though Lillian, mad Lillian, had ruined her only dream. She knew that Lillian could not be held accountable. The girl was insane, incapable of understanding consequence. Still, her art had soul, and her singing voice was sweet and pure. She was a gift, as her father used to say.

Abraham, who never once asked for Lillian, broached psychosurgery numerous times. Each time Chastity refused, despite the pain her brother's condition brought her and the small bitter part of her that whispered that she had suffered more than he, for he would recover, while she would never inhabit 62 Orchard Street again.

"She's our sister," she said. "Think of the risk — You know Father would not have approved."

"Don't let fear blind you," Abraham said. "We can improve her mind, improve her condition."

Abraham became more animated when he discussed removing the insides of his sister's head. He spoke at length of man's mastery of the human brain, how scientists understood the blood-brain barrier, the nervous system, the cerebral cortex — all the marvels of the mind. Their father was a man of a past generation, and the new generation had progressed far beyond the old one's quaint ambitions.

Chastity sometimes felt tempted, but she knew that what her brother spoke of was a gamble. And he lost when he gambled, despite all his talk of risk and great steps forward.

By early spring Abraham had mostly healed, and he wore the scars above his left eye as if the pink flesh imparted wisdom. After dinner he and Chastity discussed household matters — mostly finances, which were fair, but after his long convalescence, not as good as hoped. When he felt well enough, he took a short walk, and people who encountered him on the streets thought he'd aged by ten years. Miss Stein, who after decades of feeding stray dogs had at last purchased a white, curly haired one, stopped to chat with him. She swore he looked exactly like his father, and she stood firm in her assertion, even though John, who saw Abraham far more often from his saloon across the street, disagreed. In addition, Mr. Landers had been overheard to say that the doctor had come by the pharmacy to collect some medicines and was so pale and thin that he resembled his sister more than anyone else. The mad sister, not the coldhearted one.

Abraham admitted to feeling well, and after one of his evening strolls — the days were beginning to feel warm, and he'd been back in New York for just over a year — he announced to his sister Chastity, "Hilda and I are to be married. I'd like her to live with us."

Chastity looked up from the drop scone recipe she was committing to paper. Depression had made her forgetful, and she'd failed to add sugar to the dough the last time she'd prepared it; the time before she'd doubled the salt and flour. She set down her work, attempted a smile. She'd long believed her brother would marry Hilda and that only the accident postponed the union this long.

"I'll tell Lillian," she said.

"No need."

Abraham spoke to Lillian, but only infrequently, and he never let her wander through his office anymore. Her madness was a threat, not so much to him, but to a gentle-woman. Chastity overheard her brother whisper this to Hilda, and had he not spoken into his beloved's ear, Chastity might have contradicted him. But his words were not meant for her, and so she remained silent.

"I worry about you, dear sister. You've not been yourself for some time — not since the incident at Orchard Street."

"I miss the house."

"I've arranged for you to spend a week in the countryside. After all this — caring for Lillian and me on your own."

"I insist," he added, before Chastity could protest. "Hilda will help me with Lillian, and once you're back and rested, we can reopen the practice."

THE DAY AFTER she learned of her brother's engagement, Chastity left for the Finger Lakes, where she spent a miserable week comparing the grounds of the guesthouse to those of the old Orchard Street home.

By the time Chastity returned, all of Eighteenth Street knew about Lillian's surgery. Abraham had taken a stroll with his mad sister, whose hair was too short to cover the line of holes he'd drilled into her skull. Children, who had grown up with warnings about Lillian, followed the two siblings around, at once curious and horrified by the sister's unexpected and ghostly appearance.

John rushed out of his saloon to invite the two siblings in for a hot tea on the house, and he learned firsthand about the Swiss cure for violence, and that Abraham had performed it on Lillian as a gift to her and his wife to be, who would live safe from the injuries he himself had suffered.

"A few bits of her brain were diseased, and he knew what to remove," people marveled. Mrs. Landers interviewed him for her newsletter. Abraham spoke at length about his procedure, a modified version of the one his mentor, Doctor Gottlieb Burckhardt, used with great success in Europe.

"How amazing," Miss Stein said, and others echoed her

sentiment: "How docile she is now," and "Mark my words, that young man will be known far and wide."

No one expected Chastity to react as she did, even though everyone knew she was cold and distant. When the returning sister set eyes on Lillian, she screamed at her brother so loudly Miss Harding could hear from next door: "You lied to me! You murdered her!" — despite the fact that Lillian was very much alive, as Abraham pointed out.

"She's gentle as a lamb," Abraham said. He clapped his hands in front of Lillian's face to demonstrate that the madwoman no longer tried to bite him. "All I did was remove the sick part of her brain, the part that was — look at me." He pointed to the scar on his forehead. "What more do you need?"

Lillian showed little interest in the argument. She had begun to wet herself, and she no longer cared for painting or song, but otherwise she appeared, at least to the neighbors who'd been fortunate to catch a glimpse of her both before and after the surgery, unchanged. Only Chastity maintained that her sister's soul was gone, even going so far as to say that she had no sister and no brother either, as Abraham was a liar and a murderer. Most people thought she was upset that he'd done the surgery without her consent, or perhaps jealous of her brother's success, and that she'd come round in time. But matters between the siblings only worsened when Lillian in fact did die three months later.

Even at Lillian's funeral, people whispered that she was better off underground. Mrs. Chadwick noted that she had womanly ways, despite her madness, and it was best she hadn't had children. Blind Miss Harding, who came to the cemetery though she had not been invited, said that the girl was very like her father, God rest his soul.

The siblings stood apart from the others, side by side, though they did not speak. Abraham cried more than anyone, and Chastity didn't cry at all, and everyone was reminded of how unmoved she'd been when her father died. She'd bought a new black dress for the funeral, and it fit her well. The older women shook their heads and called it indecent, showing off her figure at a time like this. Abraham wore his Swiss trousers and Swiss glasses and a long, dark jacket he'd found in his father's closet. Hilda, his fiancée, thought he looked smart, but most everyone else saw only his pale, almost translucent skin. "He looks like a ghost," they said.

John's Saloon shut down the next year, and the Steenwycks gossip began to fade with it. Abraham married Hilda, and they had one son who surprised everyone who knew the family with his poor academic marks. Chastity ran off with Joseph Miller. Common wisdom said that she was desperate to get away, and that he wanted her for her money, what little she had. Lillian, mad Lillian, who'd been given a puppy before she died because she was no longer violent, came up only when people discussed matters beyond their control, like the Great War or the price of gold, and then everyone would shake their heads and call all men vain and powerless, and agree that God granted everyone a nature and medicine couldn't alter that.

Abraham was fifty-six when psychosurgery became well known, and thousands of people were given what they called lobotomies. He was furious, then bitter because no one credited him for his early work. None of the neighbors noticed or recalled that Lillian had died, or that her violence had been cured, or that Abraham had ever had anything to do with the procedure.

Chastity thought of her brother when she read of Doctor Walter Freeman's lobotomies on the front page of the *New York Times*. She had just baked an apple pie, and the flat she shared with her husband smelled of nutmeg and cinnamon. Her hair had grayed, and arthritis crippled her left hand. Perhaps Abraham had been right, she decided. The article spoke highly of the new surgery, and popular opinion never strayed too far from the truth. Perhaps Abraham had been ahead of his time, and she'd been too small-minded to recognize progress and the sacrifice it required.

She considered calling him. She imagined his voice, her apology, the moments of awkward silence. She had discarded her family photographs, but when she closed her eyes she could picture a boy of ten with hair cropped close: Abraham brewing remedies from sugar and soap, a mixture to cleanse his system. He'd torn a pocket, and fine white grains of sweetener spilled out in a trail behind him. This boy had grown into a man, but she could not remember him, or his glasses, or his fashionable suits.

A Spoonful Makes You Fertile

When Dvoirah Chernikovsky married, she changed her name to Dora Steenwycks, and for three months she aged into the appellation, pronouncing it daily before a mirror. Dora Steenwycks, her dark hair combed away from her forehead, pin curls framing high cheekbones, dark brows, and wide-spaced eyes. Dora Steenwycks. She felt lovely in the name, defined by it, fully grown and self-determined. Of course, her father had not uttered a word to her since the day she announced her wedding plans, and her mother, who spoke nothing but Yiddish despite the ten years she'd lived in New York, never ventured to the West Side. But these were easy sacrifices, distances Dora had longed for throughout childhood, a separation between the Old World, which her parents desperately clung to, and the New.

The new Dora never wore home-sewn clothing or mis-sized shoes stuffed with newspaper, never admitted that English was not her first language, though discerning listeners could tell, never ate herring or shopped at a pushcart, never discussed which young men and women should meet and marry and how she'd facilitate the union. For seventeen years, Dvoirah had only wanted what she was now: Dora, married to a man who wore faded dungarees and white cotton shirts and smelled of steel and dug soil. Hair thin and brown, eyes blue, chest as wide and strong as the buildings he woke at dawn each day to build, Stew was America. Every breath smelled of red meat and potatoes — baked, not boiled — roasts, pies, chicken — whole and basted — green beans. Dora was learning to cook for him. She savored her new rituals, and he savored her meals, or at least he had when they first married. Now as she watched him eat, she could see his distaste, his eyes lowered, avoiding hers.

"Bit raw in the middle," he said, bent over a plate of meat loaf and gravy. Dusk light colored the table a warm brown, almost red, and the bars of the chairs cast long shadows on the hardwood floor. She no longer covered the table with cloth and rarely lit candles. Meals had become little more than a time to replenish, to soothe hunger before sleeping or leaving for work.

"You're used to it overdone." She'd mixed the bread crumbs and meat early that morning, waited until six o'clock to bake it along with an apple pie. Stew hadn't returned before seven since he'd taken the job with Starrett Brothers. He was building the Empire State Building — the tallest structure in the world, and as foreman his responsibilities kept him away often. But the work was good, particularly now. Dora would never complain when so many others could not afford clothes for their children, or proper meals, or rent, leaving her guiltily concealing the roast in her shopping basket. Stew worked hard, which was why her kitchen was twice the size of her mother's and why her windows looked out to the street instead of a ventilation shaft.

"Food made with love always tastes good," Stew said, the expression grown stale. Yet Dora expected affirmation, required it almost, just as she needed to hear Stew's heartbeat at night or his cough in the morning before he went out to smoke a cigarette. These were the things that defined him, that made him real, solid, a part of her life.

She reached to take the plate from her husband. "There's more in the oven," she said. "It will only take a minute."

"You do too much." He rested an open palm on her arm. "You needn't work. We're getting by."

"It's not that." The crate of cut fabric sat in the living room awaiting her embroidered flowers. She'd left the stitchwork unfinished, laid out on the floor. Most of the day she'd spent in the coffee shop on the corner of Sixty-seventh Street. She carried a book, but usually she just listened:

a mother and daughter exchanged marital advice (*conceive the child first — if he knows in advance, he'll say no*); two army veterans discussed gout (*a pinch of ground-up autumn crocus will ease the pain*); a pair of lovers shared a cup of coffee and made plans for the night (*a walk past the sheep in Central Park, something inexpensive*). How the conversations fascinated Dora! Her lips moved around overheard words as she silently repeated them, imagining that her life required such expressions.

"I thought you'd be later," she said, hoping Stew would understand the raw dinner.

"I'm going out with the boys tonight." He wiped his lips with a cloth napkin and folded an arm across the empty tabletop. "Just tonight."

Dora tried to smile. She hated that he drank, hidden away in a basement club behind curtains and locked doors and secret knocks and passwords. But more than that, she hated the time he spent away. She'd spoken to no one that day.

"What do the other wives do?" she said. The American wives, the wives who grew up with American parents, who knew how to add Worcestershire sauce to a dish without measuring. What did they do?

"Temperance society," he said, stretching to kiss her. "Though the law's on your side now."

"I'm not on a side."

"No? I wouldn't have guessed it from your face. Why don't you join them? You just need to bring sweets, that's what I hear. And gossip."

Gossip was something Dora's mother engaged in, knitting a loose blanket of rumor and tossing it around like a thick quilt, something warm and substantial. Gossip was for old women, women who lived within four city blocks and pretended the world was flat and square and ended at the kosher diner on East Broadway. Gossip terrified Dora, reminded her of the isolation, the immigrant enclave she had escaped. Yet after dinner she donned a good dress, green cotton, narrow at the waist, with a matching hat and jacket and took a tin of toffee, reserved for guests and thus never opened, from the pantry shelf. She would meet these temperance women, less because she wanted to than because she wanted to show her husband that she could enjoy his evening out.

WHEN DORA AND Stew married, they had no guests. Stew's father had moved his practice to Florida. The elder Steenwycks claimed he was an only child, though Stew sometimes mentioned a mad Aunt Lillian, who died a few years before he was born, and another woman, whose name he did not even know; Dora's family refused to come. Even Rivka, her sister, stayed home, obeying her father's bidding. Dora joined her life to her husband's in a

Presbyterian church, where Stew kissed her and declared her the most beautiful girl in all New York. "You belong to me now," he'd said. She felt love then; it overwhelmed her.

The first night of their marriage, Dora asked if she could remain by the window. She wanted to watch the street and changing sky. She'd never spent a night alone. Stew shook his head. "What do I tell them at work tomorrow? A married man sleeping alone on his wedding night."

"Tell them to come over," Dora said. "Tell them you want them to meet me."

Till then she'd met only one of Stew's friends, a woman he'd once dated. She had since married, had two children. Stew and Dora saw her on the street, by chance, and Dora compared the woman's hazel eyes, plump cheeks, and almond brown hair to her own. The mother had softer lines, a wider smile, and a more expensive dress.

He hadn't introduced her to anyone else, not since the day they first met at a dance, when she'd slipped from her family's two-room tenement with her best cotton jumper and her hair curled to resemble a fashionable bob. Classes had ended, she had her high school diploma, and she would not miss the celebration, despite her father's no. Only Ivan, the boarder, had seen her leave, and he reported the event the next morning, referring to Dora as a *kurva* and a *nafke*, anything to indicate whore. Rumor whirled. Dvoirah

Chernikovsky, pretty Dvoirah, had too much free spirit. She would break her poor mother's heart. Imagine! After all the years the family sacrificed to send the girl to school. But the rumor only made Stew more handsome, more perfect. He loved her, he said. Dora married him within two months and moved into his white-walled flat.

The night after their wedding night, Stew brought home two men, both ruddy and sore from hours of hard work in the sun. Dora made coffee in the kitchen, and Stew excused himself from the guests to help. He slipped an arm around her waist and kissed her neck. She heard only the whispered conversation in the next room.

"She's a Jew," one guest said. And she was certain that in an even lower voice he added, "You can tell by her smell."

PETER AND PAULINE'S home on West Sixty-ninth Street was cluttered. Three full windows looked out to the street. Ivy grew up the side of the brownstone. The door to the hallway was as wide as the grand fireplace, before which Peter squatted, vainly fanning a waning fire. Dora had met him before, when he'd stopped by with rolled architectural drawings, and she remembered his warm Irish accent and smile. She had no way to recognize Pauline among the three well-dressed ladies bent over as many unmatched coffee tables. But the hostess rose graciously and walked, to Dora's amazement, between two nearly overlapping couches, three end tables, and an oak recliner to greet Stew and Dora.

"Come in," she said.

"I've just come to bring Dora," Stew laughed, "and take Peter away."

"We've been driving him mad with our talk," Pauline said and, turning to her husband, added, "Haven't we, Peter?"

Peter reached to take a couple sandwiches from an overflowing platter. He, like Stew, kept his hair cropped short, sideburns trimmed, chin clean-shaven. Both men wore the uniform of their profession: dungarees, cotton shirt, hat askew. Dora could confuse them in the dark. She smiled at Peter, feeling close to him.

As Peter made his way around the furniture, Stew kissed Dora's cheek and promised to return in a few hours.

"Peter's told me so much about you," Pauline said, grasping Dora's hand and leading her into the crowded sitting room. If she disliked Dora, or noticed the smell Stew's other friends had spoken of, her face did not show it. Her hair was platinum, styled in crisp waves before collecting in a bun at the nape of her neck. She wore a lace-collared dress that fit so well Dora could almost imagine her hostess unclothed. But this was her mother's thought, not hers. A married woman could dress as she liked, and if Dora had the fair skin and complexion, she too would choose the Hollywood vogue.

She reached into her bag for the tin of toffee, which Pauline accepted with a smile. The other women, Rose and Elizabeth, stood to greet her, but did not venture around the amassed furniture to take her hand. Both looked pregnant, Elizabeth perhaps eight months, and Rose showing only enough that Dora noticed but would not mention it for fear that the woman still thought it a secret.

"I can't part with any of it," Pauline explained as Dora made her way between a stack of chairs and a settee. "Heirlooms, you know."

Dora nodded, though the only items her parents had brought from Russia were a necklace, a pair of earrings her mother promised to split so that each of her daughters could have one gold-set stone and a framed sketch by a distant cousin who was "quite famous," though none of Dora's schoolmates recognized the name when she had boasted of it. Back then, the teachers called her un-American when she forgot an English word and substituted Yiddish. But she'd learned to watch and copy, to fit in. Nights at home with her family became less important: her father bent over his borrowed texts, her mother complaining that scholars never put bread on the table, her sister darning the boarder's socks. Dora sewed buttonholes, "finishing work," they called it, her paychecks passed unopened to her parents. Dora and Rivka had shared a bed, and nights they shared stories. Rivka told tales of their neighbor, Fish Eye, who traveled the world in a tall pair of boots and peeked at young girls through open windows. Dora made up adventures of an American boy who lived in the subway station and ate bugs, though he was really a president.

"It is good to have something to fall back on these days," Pauline said, guiding Dora deeper into the parlor. "I'd sell it all — even my mother's wedding dress — to feed the children."

"You have children?" Dora blushed, regretting the question immediately. She should have known this about her hostess or had the good sense to keep quiet.

Pauline nodded. "Two."

Dora sat, crossed one knee over the other, and rested her hands on her legs. She tried to piece together the conversation her arrival had interrupted.

The larger of the two pregnant women, Elizabeth, her dress a thick, dusty curtain around her abdomen, had been holding forth on some sort of illness. Fatigue? Morning sickness? She did not summarize the symptoms for Dora, but she did turn to her as she continued her story. As she spoke, she rubbed her belly, almost as if the rounded form belonged to a lap cat, a surprisingly soft, warm thing.

"I've felt much better since I began taking it. One glass a day. And it's not so expensive when you compare the cost to Carlsbad or Wiesbaden, which," she added hastily, "we could never afford."

Pauline turned to Dora. "The Revigator," she explained kindly, offering the plate of sandwiches — canned ham, sliced thin. "Elizabeth purchased a Radium Ore Revigator."

"Have you seen them?" Elizabeth asked, addressing Dora now as well. "They're quite pretty, really, a pottery crock, lovely glaze, small enough to fit in a cabinet, though I prefer to keep it out on the tabletop."

"No," Dora took a sandwich, though she could not imagine eating it, even now that she no longer adhered to the laws of *kashruth*. She didn't want to draw attention to herself. Stew had assured her that no friend of his would say the things she'd overheard that second night of their marriage, but the words still hung in her thoughts.

"Inside they're lined with radium," Elizabeth continued, "and the water absorbs it. You can taste the radiation, almost like anise. Do you like licorice? I adore it. And it has the most wondrous curative properties."

"It travels throughout the body," Rose added. She had a foreign accent, one Dora noticed but could not place. A narrow stretch of white cloth-covered buttons ran from her neck to her hips. "And cures all impurities. It's a wonder for rheumatism and gout, though we're all far too young to know!"

"Of course!" Pauline said. "But we have other complaints. Does it help for cramps? Headache?"

Elizabeth nodded, and Rose confirmed in her oddly inflected voice. "Everything."

Pauline turned to Dora, "Rose's husband is a doctor."

"It's how I got pregnant," Rose said. "We were having no luck till we started."

"Pregnant," Dora echoed, feeling obliged to participate in the conversation. "Stew doesn't want children till the economy's better." At once, she felt rude, insulting. She should merely have listened, as she did in the café.

"You *are* brave to have children now," Pauline said graciously. "It's been very hard on us, and we have only two."

Dora nibbled the crust of her sandwich. Her father had scarcely made a living teaching Hebrew before the market crashed, and her parents had three boarders as of the last time she saw Rivka nearly a month earlier. Rivka would not take money, forcing angry Yiddish words from Dora's lips — words she'd sworn never again to utter. She was an American now. Look! She sat among American women! She no longer had to sneak out of the house or wash her hair with kerosene to fight the lice that flourished in the close tenement buildings. She did not wear a *sheitel*, the wig her mother would never abandon. But Dora knew that her mother was a prisoner beneath the woven hair, a permanent outsider. Rivka would be too, if she didn't work harder to assimilate.

"Even cancer," Rose added. "Inject radium into the organ — the liver or kidneys — and it kills the diseased cells. The cancerous cells first, that is, faster than any other cure."

"Rose!" Pauline exclaimed.

"Pauline's squeamish," Elizabeth said. A morsel of fat hung from her lip.

"I am not, it's just — " Pauline laughed. "We should all get a Revigator, don't you think? Promote *healthy* drinking."

"That is what we're here to talk about." Elizabeth took another bite of her sandwich. "Always seem to forget, don't we?"

DORA FOUND A whole shelf of Radium Ore Revigators at the shop Rose recommended. In fact, the store sold nothing but radium cures: a Vigoradium, a Standard Radium Emanator, a Health Fountain, the Radium Apparatus, and the Lifetime Radium Water Jug. Glass cabinets filled with bottles of radium tonics, tablets, and creams lined every wall of the shop. The Ra-Tor Plac, encased in cherrywood, promised to perfectly radiate water with its rays, while the Linarium, which came with a special offer coupon, would instantly sooth sore muscles. The shop was new and clean, the walls and floor so white that the daylight seemed brighter inside than out.

"May I help you?" The clerk, a short man with a pleasant smile and dark hair on his knuckles, handed Dora a glass of water. "On the house," he said. "You're looking a little peaked."

"I'm not ill," Dora said. She'd walked to the shop, two

miles, perhaps. The early-spring wind blew through the avenues, gaining speed and strength and striking her skin like a castigatory slap. The night before, she dreamed that Stew's mother had called him, and he packed a day bag and slipped out the front window. Waking alone, Dora carried the nightmare into the day, and it took many minutes before she dispelled it. Stew's mother had died in the Spanish flu epidemic when Stew was only seven. He never spoke of it. The past is the past, he said. It is behind us.

Dora considered the clerk.

"One can always be better," he said, extending a hand in greeting. She took a sip of the water, which tasted like licorice, only it sizzled on her tongue.

"I would like a Revigator," she said.

"Yes! A wonderful contraption. I have one at home." The clerk gestured to the shelf of crocks. "The company makes a whole line of products — not a complaint they can't address. Just yesterday we received a radium suppository!" He shrugged and laughed, as if embarrassed, though his words fell smooth and practiced from his lips. "I tried one myself, and I've never felt better. Good for a man's drives. Is your husband . . ."

"No," Dora said.

"Yes, of course. I did not mean to imply . . . Many young women are too shy to mention . . . We have other cures. Perhaps you feel depressed?"

The clerk's eyes probed hers. He was a salesman, the type her mother, who spent hours selecting fruits and vegetables, always complained about. What she couldn't afford, she claimed was rotten — the food itself or, more often, the salesman. Dora laughed. No, she was not depressed. She had a good husband, a fine home. When she looked in the mirror, she smiled.

"Just the Revigator," she said.

"The cures are all half-price when you buy two. We have creams for the complexion, tablets for stomach ailment, shampoo for thicker, shinier hair, soap for the bath, cream to soften a man's beard, machines to radiate the air —"

"For pregnancy?" Dora asked, the decision quick on her lips.

"I'll wrap it for you."

"How much?"

"Twenty-nine fifty."

Her mother would have bargained, threatened to leave the shop before paying even a reasonable price. Yet Dora had money from her sewing. And her husband was building a skyscraper, the tallest in the world. She did not need to haggle, could not imagine that Pauline or Elizabeth or Rose would bother.

"Thank you," she said, and the clerk extended his hand.

◆ ◆ ◆

Dora placed the Revigator on the dining room table, a centerpiece in the otherwise sparsely furnished room. The instructions, folded inside the clay pot, promised that the water would instantly take on charge, providing immediate relief to all lame muscles, rheumatism, neuritis, sciatica, lumbago — conditions she had never heard mentioned before. She waited to drink it, deciding not to try the Revigator water by herself. Instead she prepared a shepherd's pie: chopped beef, potatoes, carrots. Vegetables crunched beneath her knife. She'd made the dish before, already it felt routine, hers, a lesson she had learned and mastered.

The knock on the door surprised her, and she wiped her hands and checked her reflection in the metal mixing bowl. She looked more tired than usual, though the curvature distorted her features enough that she was not sure. The knock came again. She untied her apron, folded it quickly.

At the door stood her sister, Rivka, wearing the same dress she'd worn the last time she visited, a cream-colored sack with short, puffy sleeves and a wide collar. She cradled a cloth sack in her arms.

Dora opened the door wider so her sister could come inside, but Rivka waited on the front stoop. Her sister was six years older than Dora, old enough that when the family arrived in New York, she had gone to work instead of school. Now she could sew beautifully, but she could not write.

"Come in," Dora urged, and this time Rivka stepped inside. "Sit down."

From the dining room came the sound of the *Will Rogers* broadcast. A female, a perfect southern belle, said, "My mother said I had to go," and a man laughed. Dora turned off the radio, took two glasses from the cupboard, and joined her sister in the dining room.

"I brought these." Rivka handed Dora the sack, filled with homemade challah, jars of whitefish, and the pickles Dora had loved as a child. The bread, light as beaten egg, scented the air with its sweetness. Dora breathed deeply, smiled.

"We heard you are getting thin," Rivka said.

Even though Dora had moved uptown, she could not escape the reach of her mother's gossip circle: old women, whose heads bobbed sadly, sharing tales of past and present, united only by troubles. Ivan's lost job, the Cossacks who plundered his garment shop in Ostrog, the rising price of fish, the synagogue destroyed in Gusyatin the night before the boat left, the daughter, Dvoirah, who married a *shaygetz*. The others felt pity for Dora's mother, for her loss. What daughter would treat her family so?

"You tell them I'm well." Dora poured water for Rivka, cut the bread, which she offered, though her sister did not accept.

"Are you well?" Rivka's large brown eyes had faint lines

on either side. Already she looked more like their mother. Her cheeks had the same tightness, high cheekbones protruding as if seeking escape. Her hair had lines of gray; her lips turned downward. She looked old.

"How's Father?" Dora asked.

"The same."

"Mother?"

"She misses you. You should visit."

Dora nodded, though she knew that she would not return to the old flat or endure the neighbor's stares, or her father's sworn silence. Hester Street was a memory, fading.

"Try the water," Dora said. "It has radium in it."

"I'm not thirsty."

"It cures everything."

"I've heard. We hear the same news downtown." Rivka held her cup of water up, observing it. "What do you have that needs curing?"

The flat felt oddly silent, the space too large for the sisters who, growing up, had shared a single dim room. A thick curtain had shielded them from the boarders: Bais, who snored louder than a whistling kettle; Akiva, who liked to scold the girls for no reason; Ivan, who always ate more than his share. Now even the dining table seemed immense, pushing the sisters far apart. Dora did not need this space, could not fill it. She chewed the challah. Seeing Rivka made her feel selfish. How could she have left home for an empty, unknown place? Guilt stole the flavor from her mother's bread. Her family could not afford this gift, should not send food when they struggled to provide for themselves.

What do you have that needs curing? With the question came dusk, and night would soon follow. Dora would take her new tonic, await her new husband, serve dinner, clean dishes, and retire. What did she have that needs curing?

"I'm pregnant," she lied, looking away.

"*Mazaltov,*" Rivka said, raising her glass and tipping it to her lips. She smiled, though Dora felt that her sister knew the lie for what it was, nothing, a wish, a dream, a hasty answer to a question she could not otherwise answer. "Congratulations."

"It's a secret," Dora said. She already saw the girl, dark hair pulled back in a braid, in the kitchen with a bowl, a book, a necklace — counting the gold links of the chain.

When Rivka left, she hugged Dora and promised to come again soon, just as she had a month before.

"*Zayt gezunt,*" she said. Be well.

STEW SAID HE ached when Dora asked about his day over dinner. He'd lifted more than ten men did, he said, and his muscles were tighter than fastened bolts. Dora felt the tissue rising knotted and hard beneath his white shirt.

"Have some water," she said.

Together she and Stew drank water, he reading the instructions, she explaining that Rose and Elizabeth used the Revigator daily. He admitted to feeling better, said being with her alone would have been enough.

"Am I enough?" She rubbed his shoulders, the remains of the shepherd's pie still cooling on the table.

He watched her for a moment, blue eyes reading her face. The tonic had brought a flush to her cheeks, and she felt warmth in her stomach, near her womb. The little girl would sit at the table soon, swinging her legs, anxious for word that she could be excused. That girl was only a few years away, waiting for Dora to hold her, teach her, allow her the childhood denied young Dvoirah.

"Peter fell today," Stew said, "from the scaffolding."

Her grasp tightened on her husband's shoulders. Her fingers pressed hard, forcing him down. The child would have looked up from the floor, where she sat, legs crossed, counting lentils, sorting the lighter from the dark, forming small piles. This news would have upset her. How easily it could have been Stew. How easily he could have slipped away.

"He's in the hospital," Stew said.

"Alive?" the word fell as if in a foreign tongue from her lips. Had she spoken in Yiddish? She watched his face, trying to read the answer between his drawn brows and tired eyes.

"Wouldn't be there otherwise. Likely won't work again, least not for awhile."

She thought of Pauline, a child in either hand, blonde hair undone, a cloud of platinum around her shoulders. Pauline would have to sell her past now, her collection of tables, the couches, the stacked chairs. She'd have to decide which pieces to sell and which to keep and cherish for as long as she could.

Dora nodded, laid her head on her husband's shoulder. Behind her, but not far away, the radium cure sat in the cabinet. A spoonful to make her more fertile. A spoonful to destroy her pain.

"Can we go to bed?" she asked, and Stew rose with her and undressed. Under the covers, her fingers found his chest, his thighs, and his abdomen. He was sleeping already. But she heard his heart. He would love the child, like her family had once loved her. She would tell him when the time came. But tonight, this night, only lies grew inside her, filling the emptiness with the life she would never admit to missing.

❧ SALK AND SABIN ❧

A year after my father was called before the McCarthy subcommittee, the acne began to appear, and nothing I did prevented the blotches from rising and spreading like a small red army over my cheeks and chin. I tried calamine, witch hazel, all seven lotions from the pharmacy on Sixth Avenue, and finally a paste my mother mixed from powdered roots and soil — something she knew from her childhood. Perhaps my skin wasn't ruined enough for her medicines and already too rough for the soft, white creams the other girls used.

We'd just moved to Bleecker Street from the Upper West Side, mostly at my mother's insistence, though it was Father who decided. My mother hated the way the people stared at her uptown. Whatever she wore — solid, print, cotton or silk — was always too loose or too short or too bright. She didn't roll her hair or iron her skirt; she didn't hold my little brother's hand when they crossed the street. "They can see that I'm foreign," she complained, though she'd been a foreigner her entire life: a child of French diplomats in Cuba who grew up to dance for the German ballet. She'd met my father at a performance on Broadway, given up the stage for another foreign world of streetlights, sirens, the scream of New York.

Now my mother offers private dance lessons in our living room, which is why we have no furniture, just mirrors, dozens of mirrors, hanging on nails at different heights. I use a gold-framed rectangular one to study my skin, where I count seventy-eight distinct pimples and forty-two red blotches that will certainly develop new dimensions. My mother asks me if I was smoking reefer. "You can tell me," she says, eyes appraising my skin. "I see the signs." She wears pink and orange with a cloth flower in her hair. Dark eyes, dark lips. I almost feel she wants me to admit to it. "No," I say, and she says, "Do I have to talk to your father?"

My father has the last word on everything, though since we've moved, he's become more accommodating — allowing a small black-and-white TV, the orange and blue molding Mother painted despite the no-alterations clause in the lease, and several late dinners at nearby restaurants. I like to think he is trying to make things better for us, but his allowances feel so fragile, I don't want to consider them for fear they will disappear.

For a while, right after the hearings, Father wouldn't allow us out at all. But that was before we moved, and long before Jack. My mother sees Jack only when Father's working. It's her secret, and ours, me and my brother. My father has his work; we have Jack Steenwycks, or someone like Jack. First we had Uncle Stew, later Uncle Nathan, and then — my mother stopped using prefixes — Walter, Scott, and Jack. Each one came with presents: ice cream sundaes, trips to Coney Island, a card trick where twos turned to aces and aces became queens, a box of hard candies, a carved wooden train we still keep hidden beneath my brother's bed, a cloth doll I left out in the street. Jack has the debates, which he moderates himself, pitting my brother against me on topics like syphilis and malaria: which is the worse disease? Or medical care during wartime: should the soldier or general receive care first? He asks questions, and Mother asks questions, too. Simple things like "Is blood blue," or "What if we had no bandages" — things that could never be true, and thus make us feel smarter.

When Jack comes over today, he wears a soft leather jacket and wide-brimmed hat that make him look like a cowboy. He still smells of shaving cream even now, in the late afternoon. He brings flowers, purple irises, which my mother likes, though they have no scent, and he carries the ragged journal he sometimes pretends to read from, though it's filled with nothing more than geometric scribbles. My brother and I looked through the book once while Jack and Mother were in the bedroom.

My mother takes Jack's hand. "We're going walking," she says.

I'm scraping the pink chewing gum from the cover of my algebra book. In English class, I found a second wad under my desk, where it was sure to stick in my hair during the next air-raid drill. The note didn't surface until history class, when I found it wedged between my almanac and the wooden back of the desk. "Communist" was all it said.

I've never told anyone about my father or his party meetings, though I know he is right, that the government needs to change, that food and shelter and a share of the wealth is every man's right. I've seen my father say it hundreds of times: at rallies, union meetings, strikes — even at the university, where he teaches, despite the fact that communism's forbidden there. He's given me his articles to read, pages that compare whole economies to ailing human bodies: gangrenous hands, legs crippled from polio. "How does such a creature live?" he writes. How, when the limbs that support it have no health, can the body function? Yet people fear his cure. They reject it, as if health itself were a disease, something to avoid at any cost.

I couldn't answer when Mr. Wharton called on me; I

didn't even hear his question. I was folding the communist note in my palm, imagining how I would reinvent myself, how my skin would clear, and how one day I'd return to this school, and whoever had done this would seek me out and beg me to teach about the unions and strikes. The reason communists weren't more popular, I believed, was entirely aesthetic. Even I acknowledged that my father, with his long chin, thick brows, and hairy nose was particularly unattractive.

Mr. Wharton tapped his pointer on a wooden chair, staring at me, his jacket missing a button, his trousers so short that his socks showed. The chalkboard was covered with notes I noticed only then: battle diagrams and years, without any indication of significance.

"I don't know," I said.

Katherine, who sat behind me, laughed.

"Joanie's wet her underpants," she said softly so that only I and a handful of others heard. I realized then that she'd scrawled the note and placed the gum in my textbook. Her tone revealed it, and the fact that she knew I was upset. I can picture her placing the gum between her lips, cheeks wide and fat as a pregnant belly. People think she is beautiful, but she laughs like hard change in a beggar's cup, her pale hand sporting Walter Thompson's class ring. I know she lets him touch her. Secret places, dark places. After school, after she lingers at the back of the room to apply the red lipstick my father forbids me to wear, I follow them to Central Park and watch as Walter slips his hands under her skirt. She's never seen me, but he did once. He was kissing her, but looking at me. He was watching me and I him and for the first time I was equal. I, too, had a chance at winning his heart. I'd felt such a thrill then, I'd turned and run.

AT DUSK, BEFORE Jack and Mother return from their stroll, the light in our flat becomes forgiving. My skin looks softer, almost a single, coherent red hue. I write my compositions in my ledger book and help my brother with arithmetic. He doesn't need assistance, but he always asks for it. I think he gets lonely. When we talk, lying side by side on the living room floor, he rubs his bare feet together. "How was school?" I say, or "Were they mean to you?"

We are accustomed to talking across empty spaces. When I was his age and he only ten, we'd promised never to marry and live together in a house in the middle of Central Park where no one would call us names or whisper behind our backs. He still believes we will do this, though I have committed myself to a newer, secret love: Walter Thompson.

Through the open window, I hear the sizzle of laughter. Crowds have begun to form on the streets — the night crowds, who dress in black or clashing colors, orange and purple, yellow and blue, and drink coffee until breath reeks and hands tremble. I know the Bohemians. They define themselves as outsiders, but outsiders who belong. I've been an outsider since the day I was born. I have no interest in proving that.

When footsteps sound on the landing, my brother runs to the door. He stands on his toes to kiss Jack on the cheek. Later, perhaps after Father comes home and we all lie in separate rooms (or sit — Father types till late into the night), I will tiptoe into my brother's room and tell him that he is too old to be kissing men. But my brother loves Jack. He has decided to become a doctor, like Jack. I like Jack, too, but he is only twenty-two, and not really old enough to be any of the things he professes: a world-famous surgeon, a poet, a politician, a father of a little girl. He says that his grandfather was a famous surgeon, and his father before him — all the way back to the *Mayflower*. I don't think Jack is even a doctor, or that he belongs with my mother, with his fair skin and hair, straight shoulders, torn leather coat. He speaks loudly, just as my father does, but he never seems angry, and he never speaks of politics or revolution, though I know he's a communist. I've seen him reading Father's newspapers, and when he realized I noticed, he didn't try to hide it.

The first time I met Jack, he pulled up his trouser cuff so I could see his pale left calf. I was surprised when he later told me he displayed his crooked leg to feel closer to children.

Like sharing a secret. He'd nearly died, he said. And he'd been so jealous of his twin brother, who was healthy and strong and smart. "He's a doctor," Jack confided, and then added quickly, "a doctor, too." He looked sad, but only for a moment, and then he smiled. Had it not been for the long months in bed, he would never have read so widely or learned the poems he'd used to "infect my mother's heart."

"Infect?" my mother asked him.

My brother fell in love with Jack that first day, and Jack still listens to him and nods as if he agrees with everything my brother says: that the trash can in the corner is not big enough, that one day he'll have a car like the blue Ford that drives past our apartment each morning, that he prefers milk to ice cream, as ice cream is too cold, that his favorite color is red, his next favorite, green. He won't stop talking, and Jack won't stop nodding, and my mother always seems delighted by the whole thing. She really likes Jack, though she's not herself when he's around. She laughs too easily, her smile foreign. When Jack's around, Mother forgets that she's an outsider and that people stare or that life is hard and she's isolated — all things she complains about to my father, who explains again and again that she feels so precisely because it's her nature. "If you insist on being miserable, you will most certainly remain so."

If my mother were with Jack, only Jack, he would have

to become more like my father before she could really be herself again. Jack would have to eat with his mouth open, refuse to bless food, forget my mother's birthday, and mine, too, for that matter. He would have to have admirable passions, selfless ones, like ridding the world of misery. He would have to forgo walking so as to have more time to read, or read as he walked and thus arrive late to most engagements. My mother can only be with a man like that, which is why all the others have come and gone.

Jack pinches my cheek, rests a hand on my shoulder. His hair is still matted from the hat he no longer wears. "No kiss from you?" he says. I feel my dress, too small, pull against my back.

Mother glides across the living room, stops with her heels facing each other and slightly apart. She wears a long strand of glazed beads and a dress that resembles our lace curtains, loose and transparent. It flows around her like a necklace or bracelet, something she wears for decoration.

Jack takes my brother's hand and leads him to the far end of the room. Usually, now, we'd have the debate. I am too old for the game, but Jack always makes it fun, so much fun that the hours pass, and Mother forgets to pour drinks, and my brother forgets the kids who have beaten him, and I forget the taunting and Walter, or rather, I imagine that Walter is Jack, or Doctor Jack as my brother calls him.

Today's topic is polio, which I know about. Four boys in

my first-year class were stricken, and two now walk with metal leg braces and brown high-top orthopedic shoes. Audrey, a blonde with perfect small teeth, died, but I never knew her well. I've seen iron lungs with emaciated children tucked inside. I've heard stories of children quarantined in hospital rooms, with parents who visit once a week and speak through cloth masks. During polio summers the pools close and the movies stop showing. And my brother and I are slapped — by any passing grown-up — when we step through the mud puddles we now know are really dark pools of polio, polio, polio.

Jack says that we will discuss vaccines, which he has to explain to my brother. "The body makes antibodies when it's injected with dead virus," he says. "The antibodies protect against disease." He says that vaccines are the science of life and that there is no more noble pursuit than the search for a cure to man's greatest foe. He speaks fondly of Salk. I've had two injections of the Salk vaccine, as has my brother, though he doesn't remember. Then Jack mentions Sabin, and I pretend to have heard of him, too.

"Who's Sabin?" my brother asks, and Jack tousles his hair and says something like — I don't know for sure because I am more interested in his hands; he has one on my brother's shoulder and the other folded loosely over his own stomach, but I realize that his nails are long and dirty — Jack says something like Sabin is developing a vaccine with a live virus, a weak virus that doesn't grow in the nerves, just the gut, the intestine, where it can't hurt us.

I still don't know what we're debating. Usually Jack's debates have a single question and two sides, one of which I argue, the other, my brother. Two sides, with a clear winner and loser and ultimately, a single truth. Jack always states the truth, at the end, before he leaves: malaria is worse than syphilis; you should save the soldiers first.

My mother lights a cigarette, removes her walking shoes, turns on the radio, a soft jazz piano. She's wearing her good jewelry — an opal ring she's promised me, and a bracelet that once belonged to my father's grandmother. We both hear the key in the lock, though my mother doesn't look away from Jack until Father closes the door behind him, his gray three-piece suit and hat nearly the same as the brown ones he wore yesterday. He sets down his briefcase. He usually carries it into his study before we sit down to eat Velveeta cheese over toast or cream soup, something prepared quickly.

"I'm home," he says. He should not be here. He should never be home when Mother's lover is. He is not part of our afternoons, and I sense that he feels this, that he imagines he stands on the tiled landing, waiting for us to answer the door. He must wonder why he returned at all. I wonder, too, and look to see if anything is different about him. I look and look but don't see anything.

My mother starts walking, slowly, her hair falling loose over her shoulders. She should be carrying something, a box of chocolates, a plate of sandwiches, a pair of dance shoes to return to a young pupil. But her palms are open and empty. She has nothing to explain Jack's presence.

Jack says, "But the live virus — Sabin's virus — can travel. We'd infect each other with a polio that would never hurt us, and once infected, we'd become immune. Isn't it wonderful to think: a virus spreading to save our lives?" He seems untroubled by my father's arrival. If anything, he speaks louder than usual.

My mother brushes Father's chin with a kiss so brief it seems like a whisper.

"What are you doing here?" my father asks Jack, and I realize that the two know each other, perhaps from party meetings.

"We're discussing polio," Jack says. "Salk and Sabin."

"Sabin?" my father says. "I've not heard of Sabin."

"His work is only known abroad."

"Ah," my father says, but he is watching my mother. She has moved to the window, where she gazes two stories down to the street. My brother is still asking questions, "Wouldn't an infection kill us? Won't we kill everyone?"

"Comrade." Jack rises and extends his hand to my father in belated greeting. "I am having an affair with your wife."

My mother retires as soon as Jack leaves, and my brother, who senses but does not understand what has happened, complains of a stomachache and lies in bed. I make dinner, bread with cut apple and cheese, and pour two glasses of water.

My father rests his chin in his hands and stares across the table at me. The empty seats to his right and my left don't seem to bother him. In fact, the way he sits and looks at me, I feel like dinner has always been just the two of us. That I am his wife, not his daughter, the woman who cooks and cleans and enforces his rules, at least when he is home. I will clean his dishes, as I do every night, and then take a stroll where I'll meet Jack and have a cigarette or a drink, or whatever it is Mother usually does when Father retires to his study. I can be an adult with my father because he has always treated me so. Even before I started school, I went to his meetings, where I helped take attendance and pass out stacks of printed fliers.

My father chews. "How was school?" he says.

I stare behind him, to the one small stretch of bare wall in the adjoining living room. I've never told him about the bullies at school. I've never mentioned the taunts or the jeers. But the silence around the table, the fact that we are sitting together while Mother lies alone in her room, the fact that I feel like everything changed today in some way I do not yet understand, makes me bold. "Jonas came home early," I begin.

"His stomach," my father says with his usual authority.

"They hit him." I pull the crust off my bread. "Like they do all the time, because he's a communist."

"They hit him because they are ignorant," my father says.

"No one likes us," I say.

"Don't be a fool." My father says the same words he spoke to Jack only hours before. I wait for him to order me to leave the house, too. I remember how Jack reached for my mother, how she didn't move, and how much greater his limp seemed when he walked alone from the apartment.

My father takes another bite of his meal.

I DECIDE TO STAY home from school — to take care of my brother, I say, though he doesn't really need me around. Mother is here, even if she doesn't leave her bedroom.

I spend the morning rewriting my homework assignments and the afternoon reading *Jane Eyre*. I make sandwiches. I listen to the telephone ring. My brother lies under the dining room table, his ledger open, yesterday's homework not yet begun. He speaks only of Salk and Sabin, Salk who killed the virus, and Sabin who spread the live one. "I still don't understand," he says. "Why would we take a virus?" I pretend I understand and call him a fool.

At two o'clock, I slip out of the flat and take the subway north to the park.

Walter and Katherine have chosen the south shore of Central Park Lake, close to the place where Vaux's boathouse once stood. Last fall I watched the construction men pull it down, the sagging roof and pillared porch and balustrades. I watched the new boathouse rise as well. Saw the limestone and brick before it was set, the gabled roof, the new dock and boat ramp. I know the lake intimately, each landing and path, and where to hide to secure the best vantage of every small clearing.

I pull a branch of new growth maple, spreading the leaves enough that I can see.

Walter, his trousers collecting around his ankles like folds of soft skin, sprawls on top of Katherine, who lies with her eyes tightly closed and the red of her lips spreading outward over her chin and onto her teeth. She jerks when Walter does, but only after a moment. She draws a sharp breath, and I think she might cry. I've seen her call out once or twice on previous days. I've watched Walter kiss her. I have to imagine his tongue, but I know it finds hers. I can hear the sticky sound of moist bodies meeting. I can smell bitter sweat. I watch his legs. He presses his toes into the ground, his calf and thigh becoming one long muscle that collects in a flattened mound before giving way to back. He holds his shoulders up, like wings.

Their meeting ends abruptly. Walter stands and stretches, allowing me to examine the dark hair around his groin and the other parts — the ones no girl is meant to see without a wedding ring. Katherine, more modest, straightens her skirt and brushes her hair. Silently, they stroll along a pebbled path and then part ways.

The clearing becomes mine: the matted grass, the dents where toes or heels or fingers pressed. The cherry trees are beginning to bloom. The yellow-green lake reflects only darkly. The grass is still warm. I sit where Katherine had and try to imagine myself beneath Walter. If he closed his eyes, as he did with her, he would not see my skin. I lie back and, with only emptiness above me, think of Jack.

Things will go back to how they were before he arrived and after Mother left her previous lover: She would give dance lessons; three of her old students had followed her from uptown. She'd schedule them for the afternoon instead of the morning. She'd sleep late and my brother and I would make breakfast. Nights, when Father worked or went to party meetings, we'd go on city walks, me and my brother, searching for salt cod or fresh ginger root. We'd pretend not to notice our neighbors, too, though perhaps people would be kinder here in the Village. My brother and I could make dinner and clear the dishes. And after, when no one was looking, we could steal cigarettes from the cloth sack Mother kept full and guarded when she was sober, and trade them for hard candy or respect in the school playground. We'd start a new school, closer to the Village, start over ourselves.

I run my hands through the grass where Walter and Katherine had lain. The air seems different, thicker somehow, and beginning to darken, though it is not so dark that I can't see her dropped lipstick. I open it, note the curve her lips have pressed into the pigment. It is mine now. I can paint her desk with it, tall letters advertising that she is a whore. Dark red marks on her books and chair. Red, as she's marked me. Or maybe, I stand and turn homeward, I can summon the courage to paint my lips, just like a grown woman, and spread my red smile.

# THE STORY OF HER BREASTS

Thirty days after Sheila paid for her implants, she had troubles with her right breast. She was twenty-one, a senior in college, and one of her nipples pointed sideways and down, toward her crotch. She'd gone from an A-cup to a D, and now she'd begun to deflate.

The surprising thing was, nothing hurt. She didn't recognize the problem till she brushed her teeth, and she noticed only because the neckline of her nightshirt hung too low on one side. She squeezed a fistful of misaligned flesh, still heavy and foreign. Perhaps she could sculpt her breast, like clay, into a more pleasing shape. Her uncle, Doctor Stuart Steenwycks, had massaged it into its previous form, after all. He'd told her that silicone gel and breast tissue had the same weight and feel. Not even he could tell real breasts from augmented ones. The implant, however, did not respond to Sheila's fingers.

Her damaged breast hung in a limp fold an inch and a quarter below its counterpart. She measured three times, right before Medieval Lit. The day's topic was *Beowulf*, which she hadn't yet read. It was Indian summer in New York, warm but not humid. The day before, hundreds of prisoners had seized control of Attica, a maximum-security prison in western New York, and that was all anyone talked about.

She set aside the red tube top she'd planned to wear. Professor Stanton loved red, or at least he always noted its significance in the books the class discussed. Kristin, Sheila's roommate, told her that she dreamed of the professor only because of unresolved issues with her dad. When Sheila was a baby, her father left home, and she hadn't seen him since. Jack was a rogue, her mother said. He was a womanizer.

Kristin, who was studying psychology, which she professed to love, though she rarely made it to her eight o'clock class, explained that Sheila's new breasts were a stand-in for Jack, a type of Freudian thing.

Six pairs of shoes, two sauce-crusted plates, and a cardboard box containing Sheila's old bras cluttered the small apartment. She'd written the lyrics to "L.A. Woman" on one side of the brown flap lid the night before, her handwriting barely legible after two parties and a bottle of wine, which she'd shared with Kristin. The evening's events were still foggy in her memory. Had she fallen? Been punched? Passionately embraced?

She stood in front of the mirror: short white skirt and tennis shoes, hair tied back with a scarf, eyeliner, lipliner, lipstick — all before ten in the morning — checking to see if the damaged breast showed. She'd slipped on two tank tops and a white turtleneck sweater. So long as she didn't fold her arms, she looked okay. Women who developed breasts on their own didn't understand how much time it took to adjust to the new weight of a chest. Or that a breast could suddenly change its shape. Sheila had been warned by her doctor. She wasn't afraid, only irritated that her chest was one of the ones that needed adjustment.

She arrived at class a few minutes late. Professor Stanton, in a plaid jacket and olive trousers that might have fit him better a few years ago, had already written the day's lecture topics on the blackboard. The Medieval Lit class had only a dozen students, most bent studiously over lined notebooks. Sheila took an empty seat in the back. She had no friends in the class, though since the augmentation, she'd struck up a few casual conversations and answered questions about whether the procedure hurt. The other students knew her name now, and at least one of the girls — a blonde who wore polyester slacks with thigh-high boots to class — hated her.

Usually the blonde's judgmental stare made Sheila feel feminine, envied, sexy. Today Sheila determined that the gaze assessed the new shape of her right breast.

Professor Stanton began his lecture with the Attica riots. Another prison guard had been killed and the prisoners still controlled the facility. He didn't stumble as he spoke, never paused to search for a word, never stopped to take a question. When he read passages aloud, he unfolded rectangular spectacles, which he kept tucked in his shirt pocket. "These riots are not about the prisoners," Professor Stanton said, "but us. Our society and how we treat each other. Treat a man like an animal, and he will respond like one."

Professor Stanton had a way of finding themes in everything. Sheila loved this about him. He was old, maybe fifty, but radical, brilliant, cosmopolitan. When she imagined sleeping with him, he lay beside her, knowing what the college boys did not, that breasts were more erotic observed than touched. Once, just after the surgery, she dreamed that she bared her chest and lured him to her bed, where he whispered the hidden meaning of *Sir Gawain and the Green Knight* to her cleavage.

"Treat a man with no respect, and he is no longer a man," Professor Stanton continued, and after a while Sheila realized that he'd moved on to *Beowulf*. If he noticed her new form, he never reacted to it, either before or after the right breast deflation. She had to wear sweaters for a full week before she could schedule a new appointment, so Professor Stanton had plenty of opportunity to observe her chest in all its states. He did ask her to stay after class the day of the *Beowulf* lecture, though. Her name from his lips coursed through her like a shot of whiskey.

He said that she needed to participate more and that she shouldn't be afraid to speak up. He said that women needed to find their voice, and that education was wasted on the silent. He reminded her that class participation was part of her grade.

She promised to try harder. The truth was that she preferred to spend nights out with Kristin, and weekends, so long as the weather was warm, at Jones Beach. How good she felt in a swimsuit! Weekdays, she woke up before ten only on days that she had class. She didn't admit that she hadn't read the book, nor that she'd enrolled in both his classes to watch him. She took his Critical Theory seminar on Tuesdays and Thursdays, where she filled notebooks with rough sketches of his face.

She might have stayed longer to talk, but she worried that her deformed breast showed. The sweater was hot and she was sweating. And now that her skin was moist, she could feel the damaged breast, like a melting tub of butter on her chest.

SHEILA MARRIED A lawyer a year later. His name was Stanley Talbot, and he, too, was much older than she. He had a thick beard and wore torn jackets to court, to "get a rise from the suits," he said. She met him at a bar; she was certain that he noticed her breasts from across the room. He commented on them later that night as she lay beside him on his waterbed. "You have the most beautiful knockers," he said.

"Silicone technology," she laughed. Her breasts had personality, pizzazz. When she laughed, they, too, bounced with mirth. Since her uncle had replaced her leaking implant, she'd had no further troubles, and she now carried her D like a natural. Sometimes she even lied about her size, telling new friends — Stanley's friends mostly — that in high school she'd required a specially tailored twirling uniform, or that she'd gone straight from an undershirt to a C-cup — all harmless untruths that spiraled in her imagination, bringing new boyfriends, confidence, and excitement to her past.

She enjoyed choosing a wedding dress, opting for a strapless gown she never could have filled out a year ago. She asked her mother to give her away, the one unusual twist in an otherwise traditional ceremony. Her mother wore falsies.

"Just so they know we're related," she said, stuffing the pads beneath her bra.

"Have you considered surgery?" Sheila asked.

"At my age?" her mother laughed. She'd done her hair for the occasion, piling it grandly above her half-moon pearl earrings. Sheila worried about her mother. She'd never find another man if she didn't try harder. As far as Sheila knew, her mother had not had sex in over fifteen years. "Women my age don't need breasts," she said.

Sheila smiled, deciding then to buy her mother a pair. Two plastic sacs of silicone, heavier than water and just as harmless. Her uncle said they lasted forever. If a mother wanted to, she could will them to her children. Catheryn, her aunt, had done so, for example, and so had Mrs. Luce, who had once been married to a congressman. At first Sheila felt strange about talking of such things with her uncle, a dusty-blond-haired man who wore glasses, a trimmed beard, and looked, according to several sources, exactly like his twin, her father. Uncle Stuart had a nice, easy way about him. He told jokes, took her blood pressure himself, and asked if she'd like a nurse to hold her hand before the operation. She trusted him, and everyone said he was the best in New York. He had a breast-shaped fountain in the courtyard outside his office. Water spilled out of the copper nipple. Business was good.

Sheila never got her mother a new pair of breasts. The pregnancy that her wide-skirted wedding dress concealed stole most of her energy for the next six months, and the baby girl grabbed all that remained from the moment she first screamed. Sheila and Stanley named their daughter Evany.

Sheila's breasts grew even larger with pregnancy. So large that her back hurt, and she had to buy new bras and tee shirts. But little Evany didn't mind the size, her small, pink lips encircling first the right and later the left nipple. Sheila could hardly feel the suckling. She'd lost most of the sensation in that skin. She wondered how her cushions of flesh would affect her daughter. How, growing up, the girl might gravitate toward swimming instead of track and field. She'd like bagpipes, balloons, overstuffed pillows, beanbag chairs. Things that enveloped her. Warmth. Contact. If only her mother had offered Sheila so grand a breast!

Now that she was no longer in school, Sheila read the books she'd been assigned: *The Saga of King Hrolf Kraki, Book of the Duchess, Divine Comedy*. The books were no easier to read, the language struggling to reveal its meaning to her, but days alone with the child needed filling. The television kept the baby awake, so she rarely watched the sitcoms, and Stanley never returned before eight or nine. He'd left corporate law, where he'd made a comfortable fortune, to embrace ideals. Defending the American way, he called it. Now he worked pro bono for the Attica Brothers' Legal Defense, where he fought for justice for the inmates who'd been abused during and after the Attica uprising.

He alone still spoke of the prison riots and of the injustice of not a single law enforcement officer's being charged. Sheila thought of Attica only as the time when her breast had deflated, though she listened to her gray-haired husband's stories and agreed that prisoners had rights.

"Forty-three dead," Stanley would say. "The National Guard fired at the prisoners for *twelve* minutes. Killed their own men. And then blamed the inmates!"

Sheila liked the passion in his words. He would find the truth and see justice done. Most people felt the matter resolved; the inmates had brought the wrath of the law upon themselves. But when Stanley spoke of it, the matter seemed simple and clear. How could anyone deny that the system wasn't working?

Their flat, carpeted wall-to-wall in cream-colored plush, had a wet bar that Sheila used as a nursing station while Stanley lit a joint or poured himself a glass of white wine. The furniture, aside from the two beaded lamps she had saved from her college days, belonged to Stanley — all dark wood pieces that felt stuffy and old, a remnant of the life he had before he stopped shaving, started grooving, and, of course, met her.

Now and then, while Stanley worked, Sheila considered visiting her old professor. NYU was only a subway ride away. She could even take a cab. She imagined discussing the books she'd scarcely glanced at before each class.

Perhaps she could invite Professor Stanton over for dinner. He'd like her husband. They both had passion, intelligence, a dignified age. She invited her other friends, Kristin mainly, only when her husband was at work. Lunchtime, she called it, for cocktails and gossip before her friend returned to the dentist's office, where she filed paperwork and scheduled appointments.

Sheila and Kristin were drinking vodka tonics at one in the afternoon when Sheila admitted she was pregnant again.

"Are you sure?" Kristin said. She wore a loose skirt and platform shoes, and she would soon return to work intoxicated.

Sheila nodded. Yet again, her breasts had grown, and her nipples extended dark and hard. Each could feed a thousand starving children. She was a goddess, the mother of mothers, the Norse goddess Freya, all beauty and harvest and fertility. "I threw up this morning," she said.

She told her husband the news later that night, and together they toasted with champagne. Stanley decided that they should take a vacation before the child was born, and Sheila agreed, knowing even as she nodded that they would never find the time to leave New York.

AFTER THE CHILDREN started school, Sheila looked for part-time work. Her first job, typing forms for a legal office Stanley knew, provided a nice salary as well as adult company. She loved dressing and leaving for work. She wore her hair up in a barrette, and matched colored flats to colored handbags to the color of her belt. Business suits flattered her, and shoulder pads gave her command. Her breasts looked good under thin white blouses. She bought a half-dozen cream-colored bras and wore silver and turquoise necklaces that hung nicely above the point where her cleavage began. She worked with four other women, and they often ate lunch together, sharing a single dessert. Of the girls, Sheila had the largest chest, and she couldn't help feeling pleasure when the partners (all men) noticed her — a middle-aged woman with two kids — and called her sexy.

She enjoyed the tap of keys and the hum of small electric motors. But the motion aggravated a discomfort in her fingers, a pain in the joints of her hands and wrists. Her physician diagnosed rheumatoid arthritis, common among women, he told her, primarily older ones. At her age the disease was unusual but not unheard of. Was she tired? Did she sometimes lose her appetite? Even children, on occasion, could contract the disease.

Kristin got Sheila a job selling vitamins by phone, sometimes door to door. The work was home-based, but the two often met for coffee in the afternoon where they discussed the clients — awful, all of them; the regional manager, who had a drinking problem; and the other salespeople, who never showered. Kristin had cut her hair short and frosted the ends. She and her daughter shared a wardrobe, she said: Jordache jeans, turtlenecks, pin-striped button-down blouses. How easy it was to stay current that way. Kristin was seeing a Wall Street investor. She shared financial advice over empty packets of artificial sweetener.

Sheila nodded, aware that she and Evany wore different sizes. Her daughter's shirts would never fit Sheila, even the bulky cowl-neck sweaters. If the girl did not wear her padded training bra, she could easily be mistaken for her brother. How early was too early for surgery? What would be a good cup size for a girl in junior high? Evany should not have to endure gym class, the locker room awash with girls — womanly girls who wore clasping bras while she changed quickly behind her locker door. She should not have to bear the brunt of the jokes: What's a boy doing in the locker room? Ew! A boy!

When Evany turned eighteen, Sheila paid for her daughter's breast augmentation surgery. She and Evany had discussed the procedure for years, and Stanley had given his blessing. Only their son disapproved, but he was a gangly teenager who had yet to learn about women. Stanley never made time to teach him. Forehead bare beneath a retreating hairline, her husband still left for his office each morning, though he often spoke of retiring. He and his colleagues had filed a federal civil rights lawsuit on behalf of the Attica inmates. The state had brutalized the prisoners and should pay them $2.8 billion, he explained. He spoke of the matter often, though the case had remained unresolved for nearly twenty years.

"Eighteen's old enough," Sheila said as she applied a light pink nail polish. She'd cut her hair short like Kristin's and wore dangling earrings that knocked against her chin when she leaned forward. The rheumatoid arthritis had moved from her hands to her neck and shoulders and down to her hips, knees, and ankles. Stanley helped her fasten necklaces now, and she avoided lifting heavy things like water-filled teapots or mopping buckets.

"I'm old enough," Evany confirmed. She had grown tall and thin, and she played volleyball, an option Sheila had never considered for her. She would start NYU in the fall, live in the dorms. With new breasts, she would find a nice boyfriend. She would learn, as Sheila had, to love her body. What more could a mother give her daughter? She and Evany discussed cup size on the cab ride over to Doctor Steenwycks's office.

"B, I think," Evany said.

"The people who know you now are just *now* people. When you go off to college, no one will realize." Sheila knew her daughter worried that her new breasts would be a stigma if considered false, a concern that ultimately led the calculating girl to choose a C over a D-cup.

The doctor's clinic now occupied a full six floors and an administrative suite in the building across Broadway. Doctor Steenwycks had twenty-six doctors on staff, and he had more or less retired, but he met Sheila and Evany at the door.

He remarked that Sheila looked well, joked with Evany, asked about her boyfriends, the prom, her plans for the summer. He had aged since the last time Sheila saw him, but he'd gotten a face-lift, or at least the skin of his face seemed tighter than she remembered. He no longer wore a wedding band, but he spoke fondly of his daughter Elizabeth, who was about Evany's age. He'd moved the breast fountain from the outside courtyard to the lobby, where he said the elements didn't harm it.

The day Doctor Steenwycks's associate inserted the tissue expander in Evany's chest, twelve separate wildfires blazed through Yellowstone Park, the worst fires in seventeen years. Experts said the flames blackened the mountains, but no permanent harm was done. Sheila waited in the lobby beside the fountain and read the newspaper. Falling water reminded her of rain, the outside humidity.

Afterward she and Evany celebrated with ice cream sundaes. "How does it feel?" Sheila asked.

"I feel like a woman," Evany said.

EVANY HAD STARTED NYU, and her brother had gone off to Berkeley when CBS did a TV special on silicone breast implants. Sheila was working on her Christmas lists, which she archived each year and later reviewed to ensure that she never bought the same gift twice or missed mailing a holiday card. She'd grown her hair out in a short bob and wore a terry cloth leisure suit, jacket half-zipped with matching drawstring trousers. She'd turned the television on, her companion when Stanley worked long hours. It seemed the Attica case would at last go to trial, which meant many late nights and worked weekends.

Face to Face with Connie Chung filled the room with a cool, television glow as the program guests, all women with silicone implants, began speaking of symptoms. One admitted to swollen glands, fevers, chills, sweats, and sore throats. Another said that she could no longer walk, that her joints were swollen and sore, that she'd lost small handfuls of hair. A third sat in a wheelchair and explained that it had started as nothing more than pain in her fingers. With them was a doctor, who spoke of the immune response system and abnormal antibodies. He'd examined these women and found silicon in the thyroid gland, the spleen, the liver. Every part of the body.

Sheila raised an involuntary hand to her chest, remembered, suddenly, the scars at the crease of her breasts. She had an hourglass figure, firm and toned. Her chest did not sag or stretch. Last time she went to the beach she'd worn a string bikini. Until this moment she believed that her breasts had aged well, better than natural ones.

She reached for the telephone, dialed her daughter. For most emergencies she called her husband, but today she thought only of Evany with the C-cup breasts.

"Do you have the TV on?" she asked.

Evany laughed. "I don't have one, Mom."

Her daughter's voice reassured her. Sheila curled the phone cord around her fingers. She and Stanley had at last purchased furniture, and she leaned back against the black leather of their new couch. Scattered across the floor, her index cards, pens, and lined notepaper seemed irrelevant, unimportant. "They're saying the implants react with the body, that silicone damages connective tissue."

"It's just like carbon." Evany was a chemistry major. She studied hard, had lunch with her professors, led freshmen labs that paid her tuition. She said that silicon was the second most abundant element on earth. "We all have it inside us anyway."

Sheila bent her fingers, forming and releasing a loose fist. She'd grown used to the pain in her joints.

"It's TV." Evany laughed, and Sheila agreed because her daughter sounded so confident. It was foolish to be alarmed, to have involved Evany. Sheila asked her instead about classes. Did Professor Stanton still teach in the English department? She admitted that she used to fantasize about him. That he'd been the sexiest man on faculty.

"I haven't thought of him in years," she said, though she had a clear image now of the back of his classroom, she in three layers of clothing over a leaking breast implant.

Evany said she didn't know if he still taught. She would ask around, report back. "Bye, Mom," she said.

Sheila hung up, dialed another number. She had to try dozens of times before she got through to her uncle's clinic. He was out, and no one else took her call, though the receptionist promised to leave a message.

Three days later, Sheila received a form letter from Doctor Steenwycks's office. There's no proven danger, it said, though the lifetime of silicone implants was likely lower than originally thought. The clinic offered replacement surgery at half price for the next six months. The letter did not mention the CBS broadcast, but it said that certain parties were spreading unfounded rumor and that women should not be afraid to take control of their bodies. It was a woman's right, the letter said. Women should be who they wanted to be.

Sheila discussed the matter with her husband. Should she get the implants removed? She'd worn the silicone breasts for half her life. They belonged to her. She could not imagine ripping them out. Yet what if she, like the women on TV, never walked again?

"Don't be rash," Stanley said. His skin had softened, but the short hair that showed where his shirt collar opened had turned wiry and hard. He didn't want her to get surgery, she decided. His wife with the beautiful figure. "Thousands of women are fine, right?"

SHEILA'S BREASTS WERE wrapped in an orange sports bra the day the Food and Drug Administration banned silicone-filled breast implants. The commissioner of the FDA announced that the implants had not been proven safe and therefore should not be placed inside a woman's body.

"The good news is that there are plenty of women to study," the television announcer said. "More than a million women have had the procedure over the past thirty years." The Mayo Clinic and Harvard were conducting research. Dow Corning, the major manufacturer of the silicone-filled sacs, was pouring money into new studies. The announcer warned women not to panic. No one was claiming that the implants were unsafe.

Sheila was doing aerobics, one arm folded under her chest for added support. For the past few months, ever since the Connie Chung broadcast, her breasts had felt heavy, almost as they had when she'd first received the implants. Could they really attack her body? Had her arthritis worsened? She could sense the implants against the muscles in her chest. They moved beneath her fingers, like egg yolks in the sizzling whites of a frying egg.

She turned off the TV, called Evany.

"Even if there is a correlation," Evany said through the telephone — always the phone, though she lived a few subway stops away — "it would take years to affect me. I only just got them, and I love them! Oh! And Professor Stanton still teaches." Her roommate had him for a class, she said, the students called him the "old coot."

"Perhaps there is no correlation," Sheila said. Her uncle's clinic had sent her a half-dozen letters to that effect. The most recent offered to replace silicone with saline implants, and a small note at the bottom reiterated a common theme in each communication: that any legal complaints should be against the manufacturer. Her uncle had added a handwritten apology because he had not yet returned her calls; he offered to update her breasts free of charge.

Her fingers found her chest, rubbing gentle, loving circles. Someone in Cincinnati was filing a class action suit. There was a general call to women who'd received implants. Sheila read about the case in the paper, called Stanley at work.

"Class actions are tricky," he said. "I'm still waiting to hear what happens with Attica." The prison riot case had been thrown to a lower court, and the state denied that it was at fault. No excessive force or violence was used during the riots, they said, though dozens of witnesses testified otherwise.

"What if . . ." Sheila asked him. A woman in Texas had been awarded twenty million dollars in punitive damages. Another, in San Francisco, received over seven. The cases opened and closed like snapping mousetraps.

"You're better off filing charges yourself," Stanley said. He knew several lawyers involved in similar suits, and several more who would be good, if she was sure.

Sheila felt the uncomfortable weight of her half-filled coffee cup. Her wrists ached. "Please ask them," she said.

Her lawyer, a white-haired Harvard man with three ex-wives, insisted that Sheila have her implants removed; he wouldn't represent her otherwise. "No jury would be sympathetic," he said.

Sheila hadn't realized until then that she'd made a decision.

She called Kristin, who'd moved out to Colorado, and asked her advice. "Are you crazy?" her friend said. "Get them out."

She called Evany, who had a physics exam the next day and could not talk long but said, "The New England Jour-

nal of Medicine published a study that found no evidence connecting implants to other complications." Sheila jotted down the name of the journal. She wanted to believe her daughter, but doubts had created an urgency inside her. She needed to know the truth.

She called her son, who asked her to keep him posted. Half the girls he was dating had augmentations.

She called Stanley, who told her that they didn't need the trial money, and she should only go through with it if she really believed in what she was doing. He'd support her, he said, whatever her decision. He didn't sound enthusiastic. When she asked, he explained that inmates waited years for justice — that was all, he was sorry, he was having a bad day.

She spoke to her physician, who examined her and said that she ought to have surgery on her knee — a replacement; the existing joint had been badly damaged by her arthritis. Yes, her symptoms had worsened, the physician said. Was she having trouble breathing at night?

She stood shirtless in front of the mirror cupping her breasts in her hands, feeling both their weight and the pain in her joints. How would she look without her implants? Who would she be? How would her clothing fit? Her posture change? Her confidence? She had become a 32D. This was how she knew herself. She didn't even have photos of herself flat-chested.

She made an appointment at her uncle's clinic. Doctor Steenwycks was on vacation. The nurse told Sheila he came in only to pick up mail.

"How nice for him," Sheila said. She asked if she could see her implants after the surgery, if the doctor could save them until she woke up. The nurse said she'd ask, told Sheila that she would come to in the recovery area, a small rectangular room with striped wallpaper and lacy curtains.

Sheila tried to smile. Her lawyer had assured her that women felt better afterward, relieved. He represented two other silicone victims; he knew.

SHE NODDED WHEN the doctor explained that in a few minutes, the drip anesthesia would take effect. She drifted to sleep with the thought that she should run her fingers over her breasts one more time.

When she awoke, still groggy, she had acres of empty, powerless skin. She couldn't see it, but she knew. Women my age don't need breasts, she thought, though the words belonged to her mother — her flat-chested mother who had died alone, years ago.

"Did they leak?" she asked the doctor, a young man who seemed too young to have finished medical school, too young to be working on her. He brought one implant for her, the fist-sized sac grown yellow with age.

"Does it look like it?" He was busy, had another patient scheduled. She should return for a follow-up next week.

"That thing could have killed me."

"There's no evidence about that." The doctor shook his head. "No one's saying that. The Mayo Clinic released their findings — "

"How do you explain the settlements?" Sheila wondered if her symptoms would cease, if she would begin to gain strength in her fingers, if she'd feel less tired and sore. Was that evidence? Was that worth this loss?

The doctor shrugged, wished her luck, said that she could always elect to have reconstructive surgery, later. Insurance might even pay.

She walked alone into the clinic lobby. Water spurted from her uncle's rounded fountain. How much gel had seeped into her tissue? What had it done? Did it do? Could it still do? Had her breasts made her sick? Had she poisoned her daughter? These were the weights she now carried, close to her heart, where her silicone breasts once sat.

❧ THE DOCTORS ❧

I don't know my father is sick until the hospital calls. Dad threatened his cleaning lady at gunpoint. He accused her of cheating on him, stealing his credit cards, ruining his career.

I didn't even realize he owned a gun.

"What's his present condition?" I am still in my night-clothes drinking a late morning coffee. On Thursdays I usually do rounds or lab work, but I took the morning off because I haven't taken a day off in months. My daughter, Arabella, earnestly examines my lower calf with my stethoscope. She finds an old razor nick, presses it. Outside, July heat forces the pigeons to the speckled shade of our fire escape.

"He's calm now. Sleeping. Is he on any medications?"

"I don't talk to my father much."

Dad has awoken by the time I arrive. The pale blue hospital robe exposes the loose skin of his neck and upper shoulders. He looks thinner than I remember, and he hasn't dyed his hair, blond ends and gray roots.

"Elizabeth," he says. His eyes meet the space between my nose and upper lip. He tries to pull his blankets higher, but they are taut, tucked tightly around the foot of the mattress.

"Feeling better?"

"I need my glasses."

"I'll pick up whatever you need."

"I'm fine," he says.

I sit down. "Have you had any tests?"

"They're doing an MRI tomorrow." My father smiles, waves a hand to convey the dismay already betrayed by his face. "At least it was the cleaning lady and not a roomful of surgeons."

"Dad," I say.

"They're sending a specialist."

"Do you want me to stay?"

He shakes his head. "Pick up my glasses, today's paper, a change of clothing, my travel kit, and two pastrami sandwiches on pumpernickel with pickles and slaw. Come back at seven, that way I won't starve."

"Two pastrami —"

"One's for you. Keys are in my pocket."

My father's pin-striped button-down and corduroys are folded neatly on a narrow table by the window. No one has sent flowers. As I feel through his pocket, I realize I might be the only person — aside, perhaps, from the cleaning lady — who knows where he is.

"Do you want me to call anyone?"

"No," he says quietly. "No calls."

EVER SINCE COLLEGE, I've told friends that my dad and I don't see eye to eye. I tell them we never have, though I don't think that's entirely true. I understand my father more now that I'm older. Age has afforded me insight into a man so concerned with appearances he's forgotten what a face can hide.

Years ago, and not long after my mother moved out, Dad invited me to the Catskills, famous for golf and trout fishing. I was twelve and a half and I beamed despite the strange, sharp pain in my gut. At the time, I thought it was grief — that my body was still tied to my mother's in some odd, inexplicable way, and that she'd return when she heard I was dying. The prospect of a trip alone with my father — a first — to the exotic and mountainous land of the Catskills made me reconsider. School had started, but the days were still warm enough for swimming.

"Pack your bags!" Cheer discolored my dad's voice, and he smiled, but not a smile I recognized from the dinner table, where he shared stories of the day's successful augmentations. "We're taking the company car."

The company car was new — a luxury my dad's practice could afford because the beauty business was good. He showed me pictures: a wide, white, boxy thing he described as a Mercedes.

We had to go to the clinic to pick up the car. Before we could leave, Dad saw a few patients. I sat in the lobby reading pamphlets about face-lifts and the joy of feeling young. I'd taken two Tums, but my stomach still hurt. When Dad emerged from his office, I didn't say anything for fear of jeopardizing the trip.

"No talking or radio until we leave the city," he said, and I agreed without question.

"No music, period," he declared an hour later. I didn't mind. I'd never been in the front seat of a car before. I could see everything — the road before us, and behind us through the outside mirror. Dad sat straighter than I'd ever seen him, so I sat straighter, too. I counted the mile markers at the side of the highway; I held my breath between exits; I tried to predict the next toll and prepare the correct change. Then I saw it.

"A rabbit! Look! Dad! A rabbit."

The rabbit bolted forward into our lane, the slow lane. I heard the clunk of bone against metal, and I'm sure my father did too, but all he said was, "Don't yell like that."

"We have to go back." I watched the rabbit in the mirror, already violently twitching, covered in blood.

"I can't stop on the highway."

My dad never looked away from the road, and we didn't stop until we reached the hotel, where my father had a conference and I found the pool, cold beneath a yellowing scum of blown leaves.

The next day, I got my first period. I spent the afternoon folding toilet paper into thick rectangles or curled up in bed thinking about blood — the rabbit's, mine, one bloody mess where I had no one to talk to and nothing to do.

I later learned Dad skipped the keynote dinner to sit with me in the hotel room. All I remember was his insistence that he understood how hard everything was on me and that I'd get better with time. I didn't tell him about the cramps or the blood. He understood my troubles; he approved of them. I didn't want to disappoint him by admitting that something as trivial as womanhood confined me to my bed. Not until I got to college did I learn that my father has never had a driver's license and that the day he appropriated the company car and drove his girl-woman daughter to the country, he had little more experience behind the wheel than I.

THE DOORMAN AT my father's building doesn't recognize me. When I introduce myself, I feel curiosity, or perhaps pity, in his gaze. He notes the deep furrow between my eyes and the slight overbite that leads many to believe me stupid. For the first time, I am conscious of the fact that I did not iron my blouse or trouble with my hair, which is not even parted properly.

I have not been to my father's apartment since Christmas, the one holiday we celebrate together — perhaps because Dad wears his Santa suit and we can all pretend he is someone else, someone who cares so much about us and what we want that he keeps lists. Pink-faced and round, Dad wears a fantastic white beard and black gloves and carries a sack of gifts that makes Arabella squeal.

"Ring the bell if you need help with anything," the doorman says before the elevator door closes between us, and I am left alone in front of my father's door.

The apartment, a luxurious two thousand square feet with views of Central Park, has a peculiar smell: souring milk, molding peaches, ripe French cheese. A dark, sticky residue — spilled soda or a thick after-dinner liqueur — covers a wide stretch of the usually spotless hardwood floors. My father has covered the windows with taped newspaper, two weeks old and already yellowing. Even after I turn on the lights, the flat remains dim, foreign without the view of skyline that grounds it in New York.

I set down my purse. The answering machine blinks eight new messages. A cane rests against the wall beside a pair of podiatric shoes. The clock on the wall reads 1:28 a.m.; the one on the bookshelf reads 6:28 p.m. I reach for the phone. The dial tone startles me; I'd half expected the line to be dead.

When I was young, my father forbade me to enter his bedroom. When he and Mom were at work, the door remained locked. I'd put my ear to it, listening for signs of a child — a secret child, one they loved more than me, one they played with, one they praised for her accomplishments. In high school, I picked the lock. My dad kept a few boxes of porn videos, some hand-blown glass vases, a pack of cigarettes. A series of graphic before- and after-face-lift photos hung on one wall — portraits of my mother from before she left us. She looked happy, almost radiant, even in the ones where her face was still bruised and recovering. By then, I hated her. I hated that my mother could put on a new face and leave me with nothing but the fading memory of fine wrinkles. Her old face belonged to me, but it no longer existed.

I didn't move anything in the room, and I locked the door behind me, but Dad knew I'd been inside. He grounded me for three weeks, and when I had "the impudence" to ask why, he made it four.

Today, the bedroom door stands wide open, the bed unmade, the curtains drawn. I find a half-used package of adult diapers, a collection of prescription medicines, all from Doctor Stuart Steenwycks, a letter in a hand I don't recognize until I realize it is my father's — shaky, distorted, falling apart. How long has he been sick? How long has he hidden here in his rooms? The last time I visited my father, he said good night with a hearty "ho, ho, ho."

I sit on the corner of his unmade bed and read his unfinished letter. The note is addressed to his twin, my uncle Jack, a man I've seen only in pictures. Last I heard, he was in Florida serving time for driving drunk without a license, but that was years ago. *How are you feeling,* my father asks. He inquires after Sheila — is she still in a wheelchair or has the new treatment helped her arthritis? He asks after her kids, Evany and Stan, though as far as I know, Uncle Jack has not spoken to his family in decades. He mentions he will be flying out to Hawaii in mid-June (more than a month ago). I wonder if he made the trip. I imagine my father bent over his unfinished letter. I cannot reconcile the frail man in the hospital bed with the one I knew growing up. I cannot prevent the isolation, the emptiness of his deserted bedroom from infecting my thoughts, or the tears from forming and falling.

I RETURN TO the hospital after seven. Not even dusk breaks the midsummer heat. The nurse tells me Dad has mistaken her for his wife. My training and years of study are as useless as graduation robes. His illness, his apartment, this entire day have proved me inadequate.

"Dad," I say. I have his clothing and toiletries in a grocery sack, and the sandwiches — two pastrami on pumpernickel, just as he'd asked — in another. "It's Elizabeth."

I pull up my chair beside him. "Elizabeth, your daughter."

I feel large — a parent in a child's seat, a grown-up trying to hide beside the bed because I can no longer slip beneath it. I take my father's hand.

"Elizabeth." Though he speaks my name, my father's eyes show no sign of recognition. He squeezes my hand so tight it hurts.

"Have you been self-prescribing?" I ask. "Have you?" I ask again. "Damn it, Dad. You can't — "

But my dad isn't with me. His eyes are open, but he is looking past me, through me, to the shadow beneath the silent television fastened high on the wall. My father, the plastic surgeon. I don't think he ever really looked at me. When I refused to take over his practice, Dad joined a Christian charity and began sending monthly checks to a six-year-old boy named Guillermo; according to the article in *Plastic Surgery Today*, which pictured my dad on the cover, he never leaves home without the boy's snapshot, the child's big brown eyes the doctor's hope for "the future generation." Only in the last four years — since Arabella — have we begun to speak again.

I use Dad's hospital phone to call the lab. The new tissue samples are ready, waiting.

THE BEST THING about my lab is that I have access to it at all times. I can spend the day caring for my dad, and the night examining tissue from spontaneous abortions or blood from children with congenital anomalies. I can care for the health of the passing generation and the coming one.

Still, as I sit beside my father's bed, I cannot imagine going anywhere but to my own bed. We are working on the Sunday crossword puzzle, which I clipped from yesterday's *Times*. I read clues and letters. At first Dad asks me to repeat them: "What was that S, blank, blank, what?" Soon, he stops pretending. I don't ask him to count backward from five, but I doubt he can do that either. Otherwise he is lucid. When I offer him the paper, he shakes his head.

"I see everything double," he says. "Even with my glasses."

At four o'clock, his doctor arrives. He is my age, balding and — judging by the way he carries his chart extended before him like an offering to the gods — officious and petty.

"How are we today?" he asks.

"We are fine," Dad answers.

"I'm Elizabeth." I extend my hand. "Stuart's daughter."

"James Cranston," the doctor says. "I have the MRI results."

Doctor Cranston, clipboard at his side now, turns to me and smiles. "We did an MRI Friday morning. It's a standard test —"

"I know," I say.

"My daughter's a doctor," my father says. "A *medical* doctor."

I stiffen. A *medical* doctor. I am a new graduate again, and my dad, expectant smile as wide as his fist, makes his offer: "You'll take over my practice when I retire." Pride still rings in the words I spoke then: "I'd rather help people."

"A family of doctors, eh?" Doctor Cranston smiles. "Runs in the blood or something?"

My father snorts.

"What did you find in the MRI?" I ask.

Doctor Cranston turns from me to my father. "Good news and bad news," he says. "The MRI is completely normal."

I DON'T GET to the lab until eight. The room feels too bright and so cold that the blood does not flow to my fingertips. Two of my colleagues are still working.

"Sorry to hear about your father."

"Thank you," I say. The woman's name is Kathy or perhaps Karen — a young doctor who's been with us for over a year. Her team has a conference abstract due in just under a week, and they are still collecting and analyzing data. "How's the research coming?"

"Getting there," she says. "Not as conclusive as we'd like."

"Nothing ever is," I say. "If you need me, I'll be in the FISH room."

I like the FISH room because I always have it to myself. Only two other doctors in my group study chromosomes using fluorescent in situ hybridization, and both are on leave — one in Germany; the other, Japan. The room has no windows, and the desk is too low for writing — perfect for microscope work.

I remember, suddenly, to call Harold.

"Hi," I say. "How's it going?"

"Fine. Good. When are you coming home?" He sounds tired. Behind him hums the air conditioner, a clunky wall unit we haven't made time to replace. Our apartment needs work: pantry shelves for the tinned fish Harold brings home from his import store, bookshelves for my medical journals, closet shelves for Arabella's old clothes, new paint, new floors, small things like drain plugs, a knob for the silverware drawer, batteries for the remote.

"I'm coming as soon as I can. How's Arabella?"

"Asleep. She diagnosed me with mumps at dinner."

"She did?"

"Mumps. Can you believe it? The child's only four."

"She's a smart one," I say. "I'll call before I head home."

I don't call. When I view the invisible, time speeds up. Law of microscopes: you can't cheat time and vision; pull chewing gum long and the width diminishes; stare at a slide long enough, time vanishes. One dimension gives way to another, one choice excludes another. When I look at a screen test, a glow of blue with red and green dots, human chromosomes, I feel pure joy. I don't leave the lab until 2:30 a.m.

THE NEXT MORNING, I bring a bagel with lox and red onions and a decaf coffee to the hospital. Dad complains that the drink is too hot, that the room is too hot, that people are watching him. He believes that the television is actually a video camera, that his room is bugged, and that our conversation is being monitored.

"Anything else?" I ask.

He taps the side of the bed so I'll lean closer.

"They are weighing my turds," he whispers.

When I return that afternoon with the sandwich he ordered, he's more himself. I can tell by his eyes; the hazel has deepened, as if sanity is expressed in color.

"I brought you dinner." I can't tell if resentment sounds in my voice. I hope not. I want to help my father while he is fragile. I want to rise above our differences, to prove to him, to me, that it doesn't matter what he thinks of my decisions or my work, that we are family.

"Any news from the doctors?"

"It's not vitamin B toxicity." He shrugs, but his movement is jerky. "Tell me something nice. How was your day?"

"Good," I say. I don't tell him how tired I am, or how Harold lost his temper this morning, or how I haven't spent time with Arabella or my friends in days. "My paper came out in *Science*."

"*Science*. That's an honor. Bring me a copy. Give your old dad something to do."

"Sure," I say. My father has never expressed interest in my work; now he can't even read it. I study the lines around his eyes, the crease in his forehead, the stubble above his lips. I search for resentment, the old anger, but notice nothing except how changed he is, how foreign.

"I'm having trouble swallowing," he says. "Just the paper next time — just your paper."

I GO HOME before I return to the lab. I want to have dinner with my family, but I should have called first; they aren't there.

Harold has taken Arabella out for a movie and milk-shakes — I don't hear about the fun until the next day.

"You missed out," Harold tells me. He's making break-fast: poached eggs for us and raisin oatmeal for Arabella.

"I know." I think of my mother, her second face, the smooth one that showed neither anger nor pain unless emotion thrust her lips apart and colored her skin hot red. She threatened to leave if my father said yes to another conference; she threatened many times, but only when he wasn't home.

"How about tonight?" I say. Already, I'm anxious, worried that I won't have time to see Dad and make my first morning appointment.

"We eat at five."

Five. Midafternoon. Midworkday. Arabella looks up from the table, sticky orange pulp around a defiant smile.

"We're having spaghetti," she says. "Daddy promised."

JUST AFTER NOON, my father calls me at work. "Elizabeth, I need to talk to you. Can you come in?"

"I have —" I have already stopped by the hospital once. I have an appointment at two and another at three-thirty and dinner at five. Yet my father's tone, the fact that he called, alarms me. "I'll be there as soon as I can," I say.

WHEN I ARRIVE at the hospital, Dad raises his bed so he can sit with me. He folds his hands over each other, but cannot hide their tremble.

"I only have a few minutes," I say. I still carry my purse and I make no move to remove my jacket, though I do sit down beside the bed. I woke too late to shower this morning, and my hair slips from a hasty bun.

"Doing research?"

"I'm meeting with a mother. Her first child has Down syndrome, and now she's pregnant again. She has a narrow window—"

"And she wants to know her chances?" My dad laughs. "Is that what medical doctors do now, hand out chances?"

"It's not like that."

"I know." A trickle of saliva runs down the side of his mouth. "They think I have Creutzfeldt-Jakob."

My throat tightens, and I clasp my hands because the pressure of my skin against itself calms me, allows me to collect my thoughts. I know prion disease—an exotic and elusive illness, sometimes familial, sometimes not, known for rarity and speed. One day my father woke and couldn't remember the word for breakfast; perhaps two weeks later, he began to lose his balance, then his muscle control; he bought diapers; he pretended his health did not trouble him. Within a year, probably within the month, he'll be dead. There is no cure.

"They can't know without a biopsy," I say.

"They'll do that when I'm dead."

I shake my head, but he speaks before I can. "The chance you'll develop it is very slim."

He doesn't have to tell me that my daughter and I might

carry a mutation, a single gene passed through generations, a gene that might one day express itself, or not. Most likely, in my case — in my hypothetical case — it will remain un-expressed, a dark thing inside me that threatens but never explodes.

"I can't make this look any better," Dad says.

I reach for his hand; his fingers are moist, cold. I can't tell him everything will be okay; he knows better. "I'm sorry."

"I have most everything in order. The will — "

"Dad, I can't talk about this now. I have to get back — "

"You have work. I know." My father's words have begun to slur, so that they seem to run together, to form a con-tinuum. Beside him on the bed table is my paper. The pages are open, as if he has only just set down the work.

"I'll come back first thing tomorrow," I promise.

"Go on then." He tries to dismiss me with a wave, as he did when I was a child and he wanted to work or slip into the forbidden bedroom. He sends me away to my work, to my choices, but his hand falls beside him. He lacks the strength for anger or hope, approval or sorrow, though I listen for one of those, one in particular, in his voice.

"Go on then," he says again. "Go on and save us."

ACKNOWLEDGMENTS

MANY THANKS TO THE PEOPLE who helped make this book possible: my agent, Eve Bridburg, who believed in the stories; my editor, Antonia Fusco, who combed through every page with great care; Bob Jones, Brunson Hoole, Courtney Wilson, and the talented people at Algonquin; the thoughtful folks who provided feedback and encouragement: Daphne Kalotay, Laila Lalami, Mary Akers, Katrina Denza, Lane Zachary, Laurel Erdoiza, Jill Hoffman, David Marx, Jenn Shreve, Alan Rapp, Annie Penn, Alison Bing, Marco Marinucci, Eve Menger-Hammond, George Menger-Hammond, Lenore, Ali, Cyrus, and Gus Mohammadian, Myrna Britton, Roger Anderson, Julie Wells, Bob and Vera Thau. A giant thank you to the Zoetrope online writing community and to Ben Fountain and the staff of the *Southwest Review*, Nathanial Staicer and the staff of the *Maryland Review*, Jeannie de'Aladdin and the staff of *Plaztik Press*, Jamie Clarke and the staff of *Post Road*, and James Alan McPherson and the staff of *Ploughshares*.

This book benefited greatly from the amazing stories and histories I came across as I worked: Edwin G. Burrows and Mike Wallace's *Gotham: A History of New York City to 1898* provided many details about New York City over the centuries, as did *The Historical Atlas of New York City* by Eric Homberger and Alice Hudson and *Chronicles of America* by DK Publishing. I am deeply indebted to Jan Bondeson, whose books *Buried Alive* and *Cabinet of Medical Curiosities* inspired several of the tales in this book. *Quack! Tales of Medical Fraud* by Bob McCoy provided background information for several chapters. *Soul Made Flesh* by Carl Zimmer played a large role in Dr. Olaf's search for the soul; *Honey, Mud, Maggots, and Other Medical Marvels* by Robert and Michèle Root-Bernstein provided additional details, as did *The World of Our Mothers* by Sydney Stahl Weinberg. I would also like to acknowledge Dylan Morgan, whose "What Mesmer Believed" provided background for "The Baquet," and the *Frontline* "Breast Implants on Trial" Web site, which was very useful to "The Story of Her Breasts." Thanks also to the helpful staff of the San Francisco Public Library, and to the Internet and the people who've contributed knowledge to it.

Thanks to my teachers at SFSU and my advisor, Robert Glück. Thanks to Progressive Grounds, L's Café, Nervous Dog, and Socha for the coffee and pleasant tables. Ada and Dave, I could not have written this without your love and support. Thank you.